*A Book of Award- Winning*
*Short Stories*

I0563081

# Southern

# Voices

## Laura Hunter

Bluewater Publications
Bwpublications.com
Printed in the United States

This work is based on the author's personal perspective and imagination.

Editor – Rachel Davis
Interior Design – Rachel Davis
Map Design – Laura Hunter
Cover Design – Terri Dilley
Managing Editor – Angela Broyles

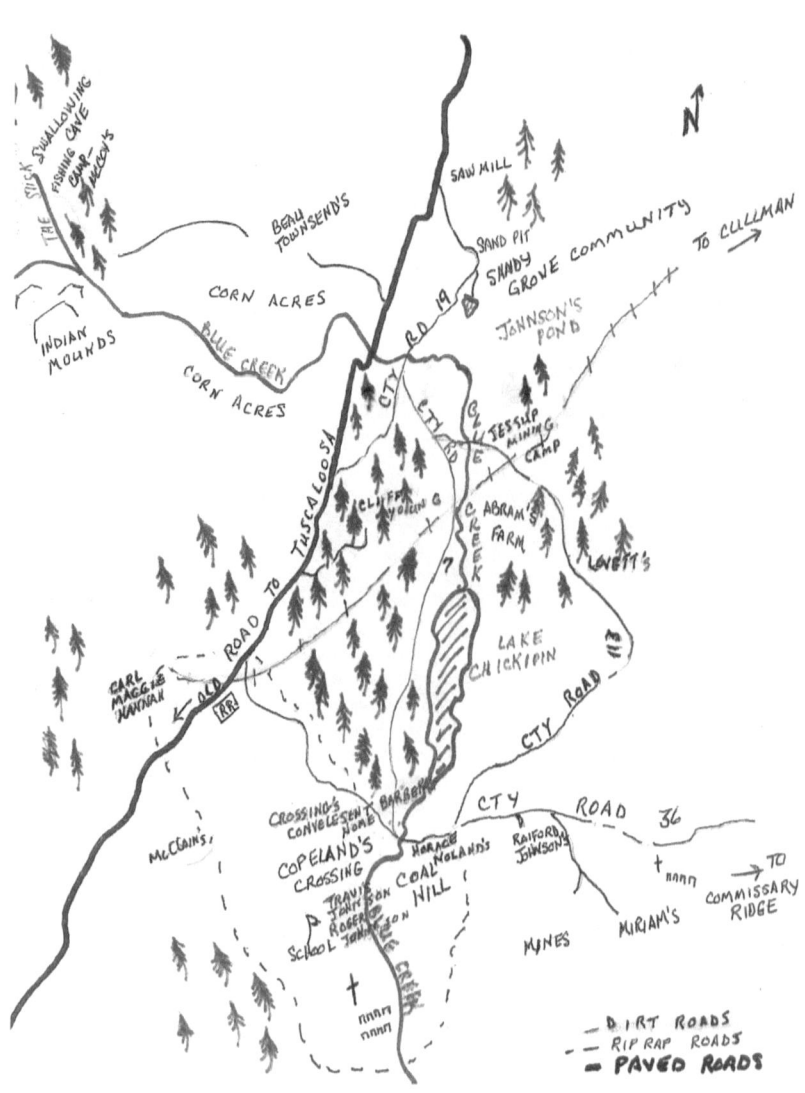

# COPELAND'S CROSSING AND VICINITY

John Donne's poetic line "No man is an island" resonates as clearly in fiction and fact as it does in poetry. *Southern Voices* tells the stories of characters and their interactions with each other through community and family.

Knowing who knows whom, who is related to whom and who lives in what section of the county can enlighten the reader to relationships that, without this information, might be overlooked.

Isolated communities develop their own social strata unique to topography and residents. No less is true of Copeland's Crossing.

# TABLE OF CONTENTS

# Betrayal

"Our lives begin to end when we become silent about things that matter." - Rev. Martin Luther King, Jr.

# The Prodigal

Raiford Johnson swore he would not come back to Copeland's Crossing. But here he is, driving back from Tuscaloosa in damp November weather. Stifled by the humidity of an unseasonably late fall heat wave, he drives with his car windows down.

Scent of pine blows in through the windows, so strong, so like the bitter wintergreen cleaner that hit him every time he opened the  primary school restroom door that he's nine again and back in the fourth grade. Fourth grade boys met there mornings to plan out the pecking order of the day. Stanley Pittman always came out on top. Raiford just stood against the wall.

When he thinks of Stanley Pittman, he thinks of her. Why he remembers her on this trip, he can't say. He doesn't always. Why he wants to remember her without Pittman barging in, he doesn't know.

Stanley Pittman put himself in charge first thing. "That pone on the side of Bigun's head's bigger than a pumpkin. We oughta see if it'll crack." Since she'd come back to school after having her brain tumor cut out, boys probed her, stick in hand, like a newfound bug.

"Bet it's hard as a rock." Stanley Pittman challenges the bathroom gang. "I double-dog dare you to touch it."

"She won't feel a thing. 'Sides she won't tell. She don't talk to nobody 'cepting Raiford." Willis somebody, the kid with a face full of freckles, speaks up. He wipes his nose on his sleeve as he talks.

"She's a bigun all right. I even bet she's got a big old pussy under that flour sack dress." Stanley snickers. "After

3

school today us guys'll hold her down, and we'll see for our-self."

"Yeah, we can just follow her tracks. She don't wear no shoes no how." A boy in overalls laughs at his part in Stanley Pittman's plan. His glasses, thick and heavy, sit low on his nose and jiggle a little closer to his upper lip.

"Yeah, then we'll know she's a bigun for sure," says Stanley Pittman. They all laugh, their chests puffing out with the thought.

When Raiford doesn't join in, a voice his memory doesn't recognize says, "Come on, Raiford."

"Her name's Miriam," Raiford says, head down, voice quiet. He thinks they must have forgotten, what with her missing a whole year getting her head fixed.

"No it ain't. She ain't got no name now 'cept Bigun." Stanley Pittman digs deeper, cutting, like a sliver of glass in a barefoot heel.

"Yeah, she does. It's Miriam. Paw Paw told me."

"Raiford's been talking 'bout Bigun. And to his Paw Paw," Stanley Pittman shoots out. They all laugh, louder this time.

"No I ain't," Raiford lies. "Paw Paw told me not to be mean to her." Raiford stops, then begins again as Stanley Pittman edges toward him, his head lowered, his chin stuck out. "'Cause she saw her daddy dead. Her daddy took his gun and put it in his mouth and splattered his brains and bones all over the wall and all over her too." His words tumbled out like water gushing from a broken pipe.

"That ain't so." Stanley says without conviction.

The freckled-faced one jumps in. "Don't listen to him. Raiford don't even live in town. He lives on some old dirt road. He don't know nothing."

4

"Yes it is." Raiford ignores the jab. "Two years ago. Before she had her brain cut on. He said it ain't no wonder she don't talk. She knows too many terrible things to talk out loud."

The boys all stare, slack-chinned at Raiford. Then Stanley starts in again. "Ain't so, Raiford Johnson. My daddy's sheriff. He'd of told me. You're making that up because you're chicken 'bout taking off her underpants."

"I ain't no chicken. 'Sides, Paw Paw says leave her be." Raiford's nose, runny from the odor of bathroom cleaner, stings, and Raiford squeezes his eyes to keep them from watering.

"Ha," Stanley Pittman smirks. "Johnson's a cry baby! Come on, Willis." Stanley pushes Raiford backwards as he struts to the door. Not expecting Stanley's move, Raiford sits down hard on the plank floor. Laughing, the boys slam the restroom door behind them, leaving Raiford to himself, still backed up against the wall.

Wintergreen cleanser had been so strong that morning, he smelled it in his clothes all day. He rubbed his arms and legs on the way home, but it stayed anyway, somewhere high up in his nose.

Raiford remembered, but he never told Paw Paw.

Raiford passes through one of several speed trap towns between Tuscaloosa and Copeland's Crossing. Though it's Thanksgiving and schools aren't open, he sees football players running at each other in shorts and tee shirts. He slows down to avoid a ticket through this one-stop town, known for having higher speed limits inside its boundaries than out, and eases his way past the playing field and past the high school. He creeps along, so slow, so close to the field that he can hear thuds as players slam into each other.

November 1971, Raiford had been a freshman in high school. Morning steam, spawned by cool night air, refused to leave dips where night had trapped it tight between low Alabama hills. Raiford has a cut to school. With just-damp weather, branch water will be down, so he can walk stones across the creek, arriving late enough to avoid the bragging bunch on the school's front steps.

The cut takes him past his Paw Paw's old place. He knows he'll be leaving in a few years, so he walks without looking, repetition having taught him the path. These endless trips to town are almost behind him. Over the hill, down to the creek, across the stones, follow the logging road east to the back of the football field. Up bleachers cut into the hill, across the parking lot, up the side steps, into the empty hall. Easy enough with kudzu dying back. Time it just right, and he'll be home free.

This Friday morning, as he tops the hill above the creek, he sees the car, half-hidden behind God's light streaking through a stand of pines. Stan Pittman's Chevy. He'd know it anywhere. There it sits, black against bands of shimmering light, the envy of every boy in school, right on the bank of the creek where the stones cross, blocking Raiford's path across the logging road. Raiford looks up and down for another ford, but fall rains have cut rivets into the bottom making it wetter than he remembered. The stones are his only dry choice.

He hesitates, then begins to move cautiously down the hill. Who knows, the car might be empty, left here from some hot drunken date last night. Pittman was known to keep a taste of vodka in a 7-Up bottle in his locker. Moving closer, he hears grunts and little puppy-like whimpers over the regular screech of seat springs.

Pittman has a girl in there. Move easy, and he might see who she is. Sliding across pine straw, grasping an arm-sized sapling for support, he squats down for a better view. One of the town girls, he thinks, out for an early morning piece. What luck. Now he'll have something on Pittman, and Stan the Stud won't even know it.

Crouched on his haunches, straining to see into the frosted window, Raiford hears a pop, and he knows that Pittman slapped the girl.

His mind shifts to Miriam and the time in Paw Paw's yard not long after her operation when they were seven. Her white hair shaved, her scar lay stark and red across the hump on her head. Raiford had been pushing her on his swing, watching the back of her head come close to his own. He stopped the swing and stepped around to face her. A rope in each hand, he stood, staring at her head.

"Do you want to touch it?" Miriam asked.

"Can I?"

"If you want to."

"Do you think it'll pop open?"

"Don't be stupid."

"Will it hurt?"

"No. Not if you're careful."

Raiford put out his finger to trace the scar down toward her face, but as he moved closer, his hand opened by itself. He laid his palm softly against her head.

"It feels just like mine. After a haircut at Lonnie's."

"I know."

Below him the car door opens, and Raiford flattens himself out on the musky pine straw. Pittman pushes the girl out of the car onto the dirt ruts. She crumples, her face in the dirt.

7

"See you at school." He laughs his bathroom laugh, cranks the motor and drives off, his dust lifting with the God's light behind him.

Miriam rises, then stands, motionless, staring at the creek. Raiford watches the back of her head, waiting for her to fold up, to drop back into the dirt. Instead she turns, looks toward the hill where Raiford lies, and begins to walk the ruts, moving away from school, toward the old dirt road home. Raiford lies flat, pine straw pricking his belly, waiting for her to disappear.

Once she's gone, Raiford turns over on his back, his eyes squeezed shut. Miriam. Picked up off the side of the road and slapped around in the front seat of some car. Why would she get in the car? Why didn't she run?

Lying there, Raiford imagines Miriam standing close to him. He puts his arm around her waist and pulls her up to his chest. She drops her head on his shoulder, her face to his neck. He feels her breath on his skin, smells the freshness of Prell shampoo in her hair. He'd assumed they would fit, curve into curve. But when he bends his head down, to lay his against hers, the hump hits the side of his face. The thought jars his eyes open. He waits in the straw, staring up through the pines, until he knows she can't see him leave.

When Raiford gets to school, Pittman's in his desk, leaning against the back wall. Her desk is empty, but nobody notices.

The morning Paw Paw died, Raiford had begun to see a way out. It was 1972. Raiford had just turned sixteen, by his definition finally a man. He could leave this place before it choked him. He'd find a comfortable place, away from people like Stanley Pittman. Raiford was ready.

That morning Paw Paw had taken Raiford's hand and given him the house he and Granny had lived in for almost seven decades. As Raiford looked down at the thick, yellowed nails, Paw Paw said, "Boy, this house is your'n and everything in it. Tear down these walls and move on to some college. Go south to Tuscaloosa and get you some real schooling. Don't ever plan on coming back. Tear down the walls," he repeated. "Leave this place. Your mama and daddy can have the land and what it offers, but these walls, they belong to you."

After the burial, Raiford tore out the inside walls. Between pine studs, he found silver dollars between the boards, coins Paw Paw had saved for years rather than walk into town to use a bank. From a map of the land inside the kitchen floor, Raiford helped his daddy dig up the X's so many paces from the back door and from the corners of the house in the direction of the tree swing. Together they lifted fruit jars filled with gold pieces, tarred over and buried when, during the Big War, the government had asked for all the country's silver and gold.

Paw Paw said again and again that he gave up Ebb, his only brother, to the War, and when he died face-down in a Frenchman's trench in Belleau Wood, that he wasn't willing to give nothing else. Paw Paw couldn't stop Raiford's daddy from going when "that egg-sucking FDR drafted him right a'fore Christmas of '41." He'd find a way to beat the damn government, one way or the other, he'd said. Hadn't even told Granny, just kept putting away. So the money was there, hidden, for when another war was over and this time, the son and his son were home.

The jars, cracking and spilling out money as Raiford and his daddy lifted them out of the dirt, meant his mama and daddy would have their white clapboard house, a house on a riprap road, a red rock road that settled the dust they'd raised Raiford on at Paw Paw's place. Some for a house, but not enough for moving into town.

Flashing multi-colored light without a siren pulls up behind Raiford and brings him back to his driving. Confused because he's out of the speed trap, he pulls over on the pavement's edge and waits. Behind him, a helmeted deputy steps out of the patrol car and walks forward, swinging a worn billy stick. As the man moves closer, Raiford recognizes Stan Pittman and gets out of the car.

"Thought that was you, Johnson," Pittman says. "Ain't seen you here in Wilburn County since class reunion last spring. How's it hanging?"

"Okay, I reckon," Raiford replies, leaning against the car door.

"Learning lots of stuff down there in Tuscaloosa with the rest of the crazies?" Pittman laughs at his joke about the state mental hospital.

"Suppose so." Raiford stands away from his car and straightens his back, unimpressed with Pittman's attempt at humor. "Hear you're married now. You learning how to be a fit husband for that little gal from up 'round Sipsey?"

"Reckon I knowed that from day one," Pittman replies. "Born knowing how to handle women." He pauses and spits. "Not like some I know." He taps Raiford's tire with his stick.

"Stop me for a violation, Pittman? Or just to chat about old times?" Raiford edges closer, onto the pavement.

"Seen you passing. Just wanted to see if you might be needing some help finding town now that you ain't a member of the Crossing's population no more. Nothing else." Pittman turns back toward the patrol car. "If you ain't going to be friendly, reckon I'll be on my way. Got lots of road to cover."

Then Pittman stops and turns again, looking into Raiford's eyes. "By the way, Johnson, seen old Bigun lately?" He doesn't wait for an answer. "Hear they's hobos there abouts these days," and winks.

When Raiford doesn't lower his eyes or answer, Pittman makes his final thrust. "Well, take it easy, Johnson. Or take it any way you can." He laughs. "If you can figure out how." He's still laughing as he drives past Raiford standing by the road.

Raiford kicks his back fender and slams the car door shut.

"Raiford?"

He stops, startled by how small her voice sounds. He hadn't expected Miriam to be in town. Raiford hasn't seen her but once since he left for college two years earlier, when he came back from Tuscaloosa for the class reunion, and she'd walked past the restaurant where he was eating lunch. He'd assumed she still stays at her house out beyond his Paw Paw's old place.

Yet, here she stands, half-hidden in the niche that leads up to Judge Morgan's office. Afternoon sun hits part of her face, but Raiford sees only the back of her head reflected on the glass, haloed in gold lettering by the judge's name and title.

"What're you doing here in this dark hole? And on Thanksgiving Day?" Mesmerized by the blurred likeness encircled with harsh gold, he shudders in the November damp. She doesn't speak.

"Miriam?"

"I'm carrying this child, Raiford."

11

A lump clogs his throat. "So?" When she doesn't answer, he wonders if he spoke aloud.

After a moment, she replies, "I thought you'd want to know. You being my friend, you'd know what I'm to do about this child." She stops, but he doesn't respond. "You being in college and all. And you know these town folk. What they'll say."

Raiford drops his head. The wall cuts the light in half. He sees only one leg, a leg wearing a sock and strap sandal, like those toddlers wear when they're first learning to walk.

"Where'd you get those shoes? You don't wear shoes." But no. That's not now. He's thinking of warm days in Paw Paw's yard.

"It's the end of November, Raiford. It's cold. And besides, this is town. I ain't stupid."

He glances around, but he doesn't see anyone else on the street. Somebody passing would think Raiford's talking to the door, Miriam's so close to the inner wall. The light shifts, and he sees her head, the lump barely visible now. His eye zigzags down her body, and looks at her slender ankle clothed beneath a white sock.

"Raiford?"

"Look. I've got to go. I'll talk to you later. Go on home now. Before it gets dark. I hear there're hobos . . . " He doesn't finish, but walks away, his eyes following the cracks in the sidewalk.

Later that evening, his body moist from the heat of a late afternoon dream, he wakes and realizes that there on the street he had never even looked at her face.

At some point during a dream of hobos, sirens, tree swings, and fading God's light, Raiford makes up his mind.

What lost thought prompts his choice, he isn't sure. He's only sure that he has to go.

Thanksgiving night just after dark, he drives out beyond the riprap and down the dirt road to Miriam's. As he steps on the porch, she opens the screen. He walks to the door, and lit by the porch light behind him, he searches her face. He's startled to see that the lump is gone, that her hair is warm blonde, that her eyes are spring leaf green.

"Come on in," she says.

Raiford moves closer and, placing his hands on each side of her face, he timidly kisses her forehead. Miriam takes his hand and leads him into the dark room.

From somewhere deep inside the house a woman's voice asks, "Who is it?"

"Raiford," Miriam answers. "Come home from his schooling."

"'Bout time." Then silence.

Miriam, still holding Raiford's hand, leads him into her bedroom. They sit on the bed and bending down, Raiford removes her shoes, then his. They lie together on the bed, like two sticks laid in a row. Raiford stares at the papered ceiling.

After a time, he shifts his shoulders. "I never touched a pregnant belly," he says.

"If you want to."

He gradually unzips her jeans and hovers his open palm over what will become a stretched bulge, then softly places his hand on her belly.

"It's all right," she says, quieter this time.

Raiford pulls the two of them together, the back of her head beneath his chin. Resting on their sides, like spoons stacked in a drawer, he moves his foot over her ankle and they sleep.

13

Night has a time just before dawn when it battles day for the right to remain on the land, a time when for an instant all living things hold their breath and absolute silence takes over the world. It's this quiet that awakens Raiford.

"Miriam?"

She doesn't answer.

"Miriam?" He speaks again and nudges her shoulder.

Miriam rolls over on to her back and stretches as if she's slept stiff.

"We can just get married," he says to the ceiling.

No answer, though he knows she's awake.

He continues. "Monday go to the courthouse. See Judge Morgan. I'll come back weekends. It won't be easy, studying and all," he pauses, "but it'll be okay."

Miriam, raised on her elbow, looks at him across the bed. "Raiford Johnson, you done gone plumb crazy."

"What'd you mean? You asked me yesterday what do to. Now I'm telling you. Pittman – the prick – he's married for God's sake. He won't care for this child. He won't be here when you need him."

Miriam lies back down. "I ought not to of told you," she sighs. As she turns away from him, her leg brushes his naked foot. "'Sides, who says it's his?"

Immediately, as if fire has surged through his body, his face tingles. After a moment, he speaks. "Well, why did you tell me? You don't want my advice, why bother?"

"I don't know, Raiford, I thought . . . " Her voice fades with the waning dark.

"Look Miriam." Raiford's back itches as if he's lying again in the pine thicket that freshman-year morning.

"I don't know what to do. At least think about what I said." He sits up and throws his feet off the bed. "I do know you, though, and you don't want no no-name baby."

14

"Don't you worry none. I'll make do. You just go on back to Tuscaloosa." She folds her arm over her forehead, and he can't see her face, though light edges in through the window. "You don't fit here no more."

"What'd you mean? I grew up here. I was born and raised on Paw Paw's old place. I'm a part of this town."

Miriam sits up, her back to Raiford. "You ain't no part of Copeland's Crossing, no more than me. You done left here once. Do what your Paw Paw told you. Leave and be gone. You running back and forth won't make us married. You need some smart college town girl."

Leaving the bed, she starts for the door. "You think about it, Raiford. I don't even live on your riprap road. I'm out here beyond that."

Raiford jumps up and steps in front of her, blocking her path. Looking at her face closely, he sees that glaring white encircles her mouth, that her green eyes are worn. He steps back.

"What'll you do?"

"Right now, I'm going on the porch and puke. Just like every other morning 'bout this time." She tries to move past him, but he grabs her arm.

"Miriam?" His voice cracks.

"I don't know, Raiford." She speaks as if she's weighed down by a tiredness in her bones. "I just don't know." She breathes in a breath so deep Raiford feels she's drawn out a part of himself and made it her own. "I just wanted you to know I guess. I don't know why."

Raiford picks up his shoes, moves out the door, and walks barefoot across the yard, the late November frost burning his naked feet. He doesn't return from Tuscaloosa until Pittman sends word in August: "Come home. Her baby's dead."

15

Days following the night with Miriam, Raiford, haunted by his Thanksgiving memory, had ridden Tuscaloosa dirt roads, passing kudzu mounded brown in winter, green in summer. Spring after Thanksgiving and Miriam on the street, on each solitary drive, kudzu hills lift Miriam and set her with her rounded head and rounded belly into the seat beside him, close enough to touch as he drove, passing cedars heavy against limestone bluffs that flank rivers made sluggish with silt, waters heated by a hard sun, waters warm enough to float bronze turtles.

Wandering bottomlands, moving like a man lost in a maze, moving through corn burned into mud-colored stalks, bared roots spreading like a man's splayed fingers before burrowing into the ground. Walking through overgrown yards of houses weighted down with wisteria so heavy it swags porch roofs. Walking past stench-laden geraniums wilted from the heat of their own slow-moving sap. Walking, just walking.

Nights he dreamed, a relentless dream in which he stood naked in a crowded room, hands cupped over his groin, though no one noticed he was there. Before him, Miriam waited, suspended in hazy gray mist. In one hand she held a silver knife, its blade pointed toward his neck. The other pressed a tin bucket against his exposed chest. The metal, cold and moist, made him shiver, but he didn't back away. A slight flick of the blade, and Raiford's neck opened. Sweet, sweet blood, blackened from blending with air, gushed into the bucket, leaving Raiford a shell that refused to collapse on the floor.

Raiford and Pittman meet on the old logging road this steamy August day, not far from where Raiford watched Pittman put Miriam out six years before. It would be several years yet, another nine or so, before Raiford realizes that neither had discussed where to meet, wondering if perhaps Pittman had known that morning that Raiford lay crouched in the pines.

At first he doesn't see Pittman, so mingled is his deputy's uniform into the chestnut colored straw. It's only when Pittman rises from beneath a pine that Raiford sees him, and he jerks at the motion, not realizing until now how tense this trip has made him.

Pittman half walks, half slides down the hill, his feet at right angles against the ground to stabilize himself. He stops by his police car, nods at Raiford, and squats on the ground near the back tire.

Raiford walks over and stands above Pittman. "You going?"

Pittman picks a green pine needle and begins to chew. "Naw." He shakes his head.

"You owe her that much."

"Humph."

In the back of his mind, Raiford had expected this from Pittman. He balls up his fist and slams it into Pittman's left ear, rocking his head.

"Stand up," Raiford demands.

Pittman doesn't react.

"Stand up, I said."

"Lay off, man. I got you word. What more'd you want?"

"Show up at the funeral. Going's little enough to ask. For her." He grabs Pittman's shirt as he talks and tugs, trying to lift him off the ground.

"Can't. My wife. She'd kill me. Take my kid." He speaks in chunks as if his words can't get past his throat. "It's different. Got this little girl myself now."

Raiford drops his grip so Pittman can rise. Pittman draws a cigarette from his shirt pocket and strikes a match.

17

Raiford slaps his hand, knocking the match into a pile of straw. A low circle of flame spreads outward as Raiford kicks Pittman in the shin.

"I'm going to kick your ass." He kicks the other shin. "Come on, you coward."

"I ain't getting up, Johnson. I get up, I just might knock your dick in the dirt, one hand in my pocket." Pittman looks up from under his eyebrows.

Raiford sees himself, fourth grade and hunched on the restroom floor . . . trying to melt into straw in a pine thicket . . . turning from Miriam, her head crowned by an inside office light on a miserable Thanksgiving Day. And he throws himself on Pittman, pounding him repeatedly in the head with both fists, chanting, "You son a bitch. You son a bitch."

Pittman takes each lick without a sound until the two roll into the smoldering round of pine straw. Pittman yaps, and, in a surge of body power, tosses Raiford off him and into the crackled creek bed.

The two jump up, dancing like ancient warriors preparing for war, and stomp out the fire.

Raiford, ignoring the sweaty sting of scraped knuckles, knocks straw and dirt off his clothes.

Across the creek bed, Pittman rubs a sleeve over a bloody cut on his forehead, then wipes his nose. "It's over between us, Johnson," Pittman says. "Go on. Do what you got to do."

Glaring, Raiford wraps a handkerchief around his bleeding hand and walks away, leaving Pittman standing behind the black deputy car.

Raiford plans to sit on the back pew because, though he knows late summer Alabama heat has the power to suffocate, he feels he's earned the sweat. He's not sure what to expect. Perhaps a one-time quilt frayed and wadded around the body. Perhaps a dingy tick feather pillow with the body nestled deep in the fluff. But as he steps into the one-room church, he's startled by this box, balanced on two wooden saw horses, this tiny box the color of cream-filled milk. Above the coffin, its lip open to heavy, still air, hangs a wooden Bible, its pages open and carved with words he should recognize but doesn't.

Raiford hesitates about moving forward. He looks for Miriam to give him direction, but she isn't there. Outside, a cloud crosses between the sun and pines, darkening the area where Miriam's child lies. Thunder, bloated with the sound of approaching rain and set in motion by rising afternoon heat, resounds toward Copeland's Crossing. Out the window, past the woods, headed for the school, heat haze sits like a wall.

At the altar, Raiford forces himself to look at Miriam's daughter. Before him, a baby's cap, tatted in circles with a thin pink ribbon tied at the chin, covers the head of a shoe box-sized baby. Thunder cracks just outside the church. Its sharpness, foretelling the cold that inevitably follows unexpected storms, chills Raiford.

Under the noise of the thunder, Miriam steps up beside Raiford. As he realizes she's taken his arm, tears tingle his eyes. He swallows and looks down at her. "Miriam, I'm sorry. I'm so, so sorry." He drops his head on her shoulder and sobs like a lost child.

Miriam places her arm around his waist and nudges him away from the coffin. She guides him to the second pew, where they sit together, their hands clasped over her knee.

Outside, pines sway in the wind. Clouds blow aside, allowing a hot shaft of light to settle on Raiford's back. The intensity of the heat, of the day, of the knowledge that Miriam would have forgiven him had he never spoken, breaks a sweat over his shoulders and up onto his face. Miriam, taking a man's handkerchief from her pocket, wipes it away.

Driving back to Tuscaloosa after the service, Raiford will drive down the old dirt road, but turn back before he reaches Miriam. He'll pass the cemetery. He will see Stanley Pittman squatting by the narrow mound, soft from burial and muddy from the summer downpour. Pittman on his knees, raking up pine straw with his hands, placing it clump by clump on the little grave.

# Sister's Music Lesson

Evenings, dressed in crepe and long soft pearls, Sister moves through life in a cloud of loose powder. Aging elegance, some say, a Dresden figure come to life. For her piano pupils, she's Beethoven's "Für Elise" personified. Papa Daddy calls her his china doll.

Last night, Al and his friends stormed her thirty-first birthday dinner with Papa Daddy. Beer and the presence of "the boys" shifted the event, drawing on Sister as the brunt of their jokes. Everything that set her apart dragged out in the open and undressed for everyone to see. Her filmy dresses. Her hair, tight against her scalp, plaited and twisted into a bun that rests atop her collar. Her deep-seated love of Classical music. Her willingness to cloister herself in a sheet music world, a place manipulated by flexible wrists and nimble fingers.

Papa Daddy just sipped his Old Forester and pulled on his cigar. The flush from his roasting glowed red enough to light her upstairs to bed. This morning she can't deny Al's comments or the guffaws from his friends.

Tonight she won't be sipping sweet tea on the porch. To make amends, Al promises to show her a good time. "As much fun as Copeland's Crossing has to offer my baby sister." He grins his lop-sided grin and jabs her in the ribs before she can slap his hand away. "Gonna hear what the 'real world' sounds like."

At breakfast Papa Daddy chided her. "You're a grown woman. Why let some careless talk from Al get to you?" He leaned back and chewed his Havana. "Get out there and see how other people live, Sister. Spending your life on that piano bench won't get you a husband." He plucked a touch of tobacco off his tongue.

"I'm content on my bench, Father. I don't need a husband." The tenseness of the conversation made her jaw taut, and she crunched her dry toast.

"Maybe you don't. But right now, far as Copeland's Crossing's concerned, you do need to save face." He sipped coffee from his Hardee's 1989 souvenir mug. "Don't think your guests didn't notice you tearing up."

"I didn't invite them." She wiped her fingers on the linen napkin she had ironed the day before. "Al did."

"None the matter. He so much as called you a prude. Prove him wrong, daughter." He set down his mug, "And pour me some more coffee."

"Maybe," she muttered.

"No. He's taking you out tonight. I'll see to it." He tapped cigar ash into his congealed egg yolk. "Might even have you play. If there's a piano."

Sister lifted the coffee pot and filled the brown and tan mug.

Al said they were going to Logan's Lounge. Later in the morning, she scanned the newspaper looking for anything about Logan's Lounge. She found it on the back page. Dell Preston, Country Music's Next Mega Star. The calligraphy headline suggested it might draw an acceptable clientele. As long as she didn't see any of her students' parents.

If Al goes, he'll look after her. If Papa Daddy insists, she obeys.

Al cranks Papa Daddy's bronze Cadillac and heads south for Logan's Lounge. "Taking my baby sister out for a night on the town," he says and chuckles. "You'll love Dell's music." Al's a regular, he tells her as he pulls into the parking lot. He drives in to the sound of parking lot slag slapping the bottom of the car. Cars and trucks lined willy-nilly fill the lot so close together Al has to loop around twice to find a parking space large enough for the Cadillac.

An unpainted concrete block building sits long and narrow against an excavated hillside, its Alabama clay creating a naked backdrop. Its sign tops the flat roof in a triangular spire. A red "Open" sign blinks in the only window. A low-watt bulb hangs over a solid wood door at the far end of the building.

Sister tests each step across the lot to prevent rock chips from bruising her feet through her thin leather slippers.

At the door, she stands back, waiting for Al to buy her ticket. Thin-winged, white moths beat themselves against the hot light and drop to the floor. Sister watches one drop, no more than a shell, seared from the glowing heat.

A woman with stick-brown hair, her bangs brushing charcoal brows, edges her way in front of Al. "Move it, honey," she says. Al grins and steps back. The woman takes the arm of the nearest man and rubs her hips against his, an attempt to con entry money. The long-boned man, his teeth a too-white line of ivory between his lips, rubs back and digs into his pocket for another five. Desperate for a partner to rub her body against his, piano mouth hands her money. Sister glances away.

Al leads Sister inside. "Choose your table, little sister," he says.

Disconcerted by the woman's brashness, she chooses a table midway down the nearest wall. Al pulls out a chair, and Sister sits. Dim light casts smoke-clouded reflections. The sour odor of beer that sets in Al's clothes and hair is inescapable here, permeating the room and burning her nose.

As soon as she is seated, Al drops six twenties on the table. He tells her he'll be right back and disappears into the fog. Clutching the twenties in her fist, Sister calls to him. "Wait," she says and reaches out in his direction. Al doesn't turn. He vanishes into the crowd.

Sister strains her neck for a moment, trying to see him. She stops when she realizes the men look alike. Jeans. Floppy plaid shirts. Some with broad brimmed hats. Some in frayed caps with logos she doesn't recognize across the front. Muddy work shoes or pointed calf-high boots.

In her confusion, she cannot remember what Al had on.

A heavily permed waitress, wearing an apron longer than her skirt, materializes out of the smoke. She stops at Sister's table. "What you want, girlie?"

Distracted by the woman's springy yellow curls, she thinks a moment, orders a glass of wine and holds out a twenty.

The server stuffs Sister's money in her apron pocket and offers no change. Sister hesitates to question the cost. Papa Daddy buys her wine. He knows the proper order for white or red meat. One glass per outing. "You're a young lady, you know," he tells her.

The waitress returns with an iced-tea glass of Bordeaux. "Only kind we got. We ain't got no wine glass, Hon. Most drink beer straight out the bottle here."

The ivory-toothed man from the door grumbles past Sister's table and away from the woman who had asked for ticket money. "Ain't wasting my fiver for no smart-ass. Won't dance. Oughta throw her out."

Sister watches the woman, expecting her to drop her head, to run. Instead, she saunters over to the table nearest

Sister. A squat man, more brown suit than face, rises and nods his head toward a chair. The woman scratches his bald spot, giggles, and sits.

Sister keeps her eyes low, her Bordeaux warming before her. She has come to see what others joked about at last night's party, to see what she has missed these years past.

Over the hum of voices seeping out of the room's dimness, a musician strikes a loud chord on his guitar. People applaud, and the man begins a whining song that mentions Jennings, Pride, and Haggard, names Sister vaguely remembers from Al. "You never even called me by my name," he serenades.

Over the music, the stick-haired woman blasts out, "Oh, don't you just love David Alan Cole?" She stands and tugs at the brown suit's sleeve. "Come on, Honey. Dance with me." She tugs him out of his chair to join bodies molded together, moving across the dance floor.

Sister sits at a table in semi-darkness, waiting for Al. She closes her eyes to listen with purpose for modulations, Latino rhythms, for anything she recognizes. The people all seem to know the stories these country ballads tell as well as she knows Baroque.

She concentrates as instruments play a song that has people lined up kicking their feet and scraping the floor as they move back and forth. Nothing but rhythm resonates with her, but her toes tap to beats so deeply embedded within her that she at first does not realize her foot moves.

Rather than sit here with closed eyes burning from cigarette smoke, she places herself on an airy porch, dressed in pink floating chiffon, "Moonlight Sonata" trickling from her fingers as effortlessly as from Beethoven's own. This is music, music composed for some nameless love. She sways

25

her head with the gliding rhythm of the sonata's melody, light as a suspended hummingbird before its scarlet flower.

Spotty applause startles her, and she opens her eyes.

The waitress is before her with another glass of wine on her tray. She places it on the table.

"Compliments of the gentleman." She tosses her curls toward the bar. "Black shirt. White collar."

Sister looks at the man eyeing her. He winks. She shutters at the greasy hair down his back and dark wavy beard that brushes his open shirt. "No thank you. I'll buy my own." Sister places another twenty on the tray.

More applause and Dell Preston steps out and swaggers across the narrow stage.

Sister's back straightens. There seems to be no face on this man. Just a pair of jeans standing before her. A pair of jeans so revealing she blushes. She scrutinizes his body, as inviting as the smooth ivories she touches each day. Heat radiates from her face, and she shifts her eyes, certain he has seen her watching him.

Before her, Preston spreads his legs. A monument. An Adonis, his knees stiff, resting on pointed boots. Dark glasses and a broad brimmed hat shadow his face. So unlike Papa Daddy with his paunch belly, his thin brown hair so like her own, and gnawed off cigar. So unlike Al, boisterous, foolish in his attempts to garner a laugh from some imagined audience.

Dell Preston croons a song so luscious it caresses her skin as it settles over her like soft cashmere. The lightness of his voice and the twang of the steel guitar warm her to her bones.

She closes her eyes, clothing herself in this new music and its lyrics. Feathery cashmere. Cozy in winter. Cool in summer.

26

"You lay so easy on my mind," he sings. His words startle her. How can he know her thoughts? Yes, if not cashmere, then silk.

Sister peeps under her brows at Preston. Convinced his eyes are dark beneath the hat's shade, she pictures them settling on her as if he has been waiting night after night for her to appear. She breathes faster, as when she, a child, had chanced upon her mother and father embracing in the kitchen. Sister slid behind the doorframe and watched her mother caress, then rub, her father's trousers, low beneath his belt. A bulge appeared like an overgrown abscess. This unforeseen power of her mother's hands sent her running for her bedroom where she threw herself panting, then crying, on her bed.

The power of hands thereafter amazed her. She knows their supremacy. Hers have moved listeners for decades. She has taught children, boys, girls, to manipulate emotions by using their hands, their fingers, just so. With this man before her, she questions if she has been right in guiding children into an emotional realm they may not know themselves.

Sister turns her head away so none can see her blush and takes another drink of wine. Like a queen, she listens. He serenades only her, his eyes skimming, yet ignoring the dancers. This novel music, this music created from fitted denim and bulging pants, lifts her above the interlocked couples and settles her on a crest above them, directly in his line of vision.

She examines, in magnification, every detail, every movement he makes. Behind his dark glasses, were she to see, his eyes would be hypnotic slits. She strains her neck and watches up close as his lips brush the microphone tip with words and gestures new to her. Without thought, she licks her lips.

His hand palms his hip, sliding up and down, a pre-paratory movement for what she is not sure. Hands now warm and pliable, he strokes the guitar's body in regular time, as constant as her metronome's clicks. The guitar responds as if he has awakened it from dark sleep. She can feel the instrument against her body and thinks she must buy a guitar like this and learn to rub its magnificent, light-reflecting wood.

He sways free, singing only to her. She has heard others say it's like there's nobody else in the room, this communion with some other world. "Ha," she had rebuked. But no more.

Yes. She accepts the sensation. "Welcome to my world," he sings. Yes, indeed.

A female backup harmonizes with him. When the song ends, he slaps her buttocks and sends her off stage. Sister is certain Dell, were he to know her musical proficiency, would prefer to have her on stage with him. And when the music ends, he would place his hand on her shoulder and kiss her brow. The audience would cheer at the joy before them.

The waitress re-appears. "Want another one?"

In wonder, Sister sees her glass is empty. She hesitates, but replies, "Yes. Please." She gives the server another twenty.

The waitress has another iced-tea glass ready. She sets it before Sister. Wine sloshes over the rim. Sister dips her middle finger into the spill. She taps the pungent taste on her tongue and sighs.

She thinks through the melody line of every song, storing it in her memory, so she can play each bar in private. She can research lyrics later, when the public library is open and most people are at work. Sister gulps her wine as she distills the music.

Dell calls for a break, and the band exits the stage.

Sister goes to the bathroom. Inside, the acidic stench of diabetic urine overpowers her. She tries to back out, but the door opens and bumps her. She moves aside. Force from the swing sends the knob cracking into the wall.

The stick-haired woman stumbles in, dragging her novice dressed in an orange mini-skirt by the arm.

"Well, looky at who's still here." She grins at Sister's reflection in the mirror. "Thought you'd be well gone by now, girlie."

Sister moves to leave.

"Where're you going? We just startin' to party." She pushes the young girl toward a stall. "Get in there before you puke all over the floor, kid." The girl's chocolate hair dangles forward, hiding her face as she lurches for the toilet.

Sister opens the door to leave. The woman grabs her arm and pulls her back. "I seen you looking all moon-eyed at Dell. He ain't interested in you. Why don't you just go on home now. 'Fore you embarrass yourself."

Sister jerks her arm free. "Keep your hands off me." She wipes her arm to cleanse the touch of such a hand, slams the door against the gagging and edges down the wall to her table.

Al is nowhere to be seen.

Back on stage, Dell announces a medley of Hank Williams' songs, "for all you love-hungry young ladies out there."

There in the spotlight, he fingers the guitar for the right key, the key that fits the two of them best, Sister decides. She receives him openly.

He leans toward her with his announcement, "Now a tribute to Ole' Hank." The music is quiet and mournful. Something about a robin weeping and being so lonesome he could die. Sister could have written the words herself. Loneliness hits her. It's her song. It's their song. Sister glances round to see if others see the desire he has for her in his eyes, if they feel the energy between them.

*Is this really me, sitting here in this haze?* she asks herself. A tingle glides through her body like a rippling series of scales. *Why aren't I home practicing arpeggios or in some well-lighted restaurant where I know the rules about spying on undulating bodies, rather than here, eavesdropping on primitive sounds in this darkened room?*

On the dance floor before her, individuals no longer exist, nor do inhibitions. Without men, women dance with women who move to find men and then back to women. In their density, they whirl. They spin. They gyrate. The floor vibrates. Music's intensity billows around her, stroking her face, her arms. His voice, his movements chain her to her chair.

Sister lifts her glass, only to find it empty again. Her waitress emerges from the smoke with another iced-tea glass full of black-red wine.

"Need something to eat with that wine, lady?"

Sister doesn't answer. Her tongue refuses to speak. She taps it with her forefinger to see if it is swollen. No. Just numb. She doesn't speak. Her teeth might bite down hard and bring blood.

She takes another drink and sets her glass down near the center of the table. She lifts her eyes to Dell's black glasses as he glides his hips to form another pose. She looks at her hand as if it belongs to someone she doesn't know then brings the wine to her lips.

30

"I've hungered for your touch a long, lonely time," he croons.

Her fingers falter when his voice breaks. Such a primal thought, the touch of her hands on a man's body, his on hers, alters her composure. Her hand slips. Bordeaux tips over, onto her breast. She looks down at the stain, a splash of burgundy, soaking, as it spreads down her dress.

She stands as he steps from the stage. Behind her, a chair falls.

He moves in slow motion through a wave of dancers, straight for her table.

When he reaches her table, she will lift her glass in a toast and offer her hand. He'll caress her fingertips, sending a sweeping Viennese waltz up her arm. Her fingers tingle even before he reaches her table.

He'll drift across the dance floor, she imagines, a strutting toreador in his coal black hat to meet her, his flamenco dancer. With short uneven hair escaping from that bound at the nape of his neck, he'll move toward her, fluid with Bolero's opening drum and evocative flute swells gathering momentum behind him. She'll bend forward and draw her finger softly down a scar on his cheek. He'll bend to kiss her as an oboe answers the flute.

Dell moves closer. Behind him, she glimpses toward the man at the bar. Still there, watching her. In her head, muted trumpets repeat the motif.

Sister moves toward the dance floor, her steps as precise as fingers plucking violin strings.

Dell comes closer, coming her way.

Bolero's alto sax drops an octave lower and deepens the theme. Sister's heart beats to the minor shift and follows

31

the drum.

He nears. Trombones slide in. Out. In. Out. She waits for the rising crescendo to roar from round French horns.

This is her dance.

Dell Preston walks past without a pause. Some distance away, he turns and removes his dark glasses. His eyes, now visible under his Stetson hat, are blue, a blue washed-out and pale. He never glances her way. Instead, he seeks out a leather-wrinkled woman who sashays up to meet him. They kiss, a full-mouth, embarrassing kiss. Dancers applaud and whoop their approval. The waitress swings her mopping towel over her head. Round and round.

Sister's eyes drop. Hot air seeps from her pores. Both hands grip her thighs, and she twirls, to bolt toward the door, back to silk under linen, sweet cream atop berries. She stumbles, hitting the chair leg. "Whump" slips from her lips. She regains some balance and limps toward the red neon exit sign.

Behind her, she recognizes the laughter of low-life women. Their cackle pushes her out the door. Wagner invades her mind with her own "Ride of the Valkyries." Successive layers of violins play and replay, building as they relinquish their power to shrieking flutes and whirling piccolo that carry her to the icy mountaintop where Valkyrie sisters wait with Brunnhilde to set her, a wounded warrior, back on earth. No Valhalla. No "Bridal Chorus." Not this night.

Her battle a humiliating loss, Sister staggers toward where she thinks Al parked Papa Daddy's Caddy, her stomach churning. Once inside the car, she will tap on the air conditioner. The night, her body, her face are hot hot hot. Her mouth is dry. She longs for a glass of iced-tea. She stumbles into a bruised truck and slides to the ground, gravel cutting into her knee when she lands. "My God," she pleads, "just let me die."

Severe hands slip under her arms and pull her up. She focuses through dim dusk-to-dawn light. "Al?"

"No," a voice answers. "It's me."

Sister squints, edging closer. The black shirt. White collar. The blush of Bordeaux spreads up from her stained breast and flushes her face.

"Come with me." He puts her hand in his and holds her elbow. "It's okay."

Sister exhales vinegary wine. "It's okay," she repeats. "Al will be there."

"Yes. It's okay," the man answers.

He leads Sister back through the slag toward Logan's Lounge.

# The Uncertainty of Light

Here they are, a carnie who, at twenty-eight, passes through Realtown, outside Copeland's Crossing, every August, awaiting the right time to empty his rage against the woman, just over forty, who refuses to accept that she is no more than a convenient bed.

Near dusk, Onnie leaves. She with her present: a straight razor with its intricate elephant handle and prime hair shears wrapped in brown paper and tied with twine. Ernest left with Spud before noon, smelly old Spud who carries cattle prods. "For wild animals," he had grinned.

It's the last quarter moon of a parched August. Papa had told her earlier not to go. "People been kilt down there."

"He needs a haircut," Onnie said. "I got fine shears and a razor." Onnie shifted in her chair and tensed her ankles.

"Devils work there," Papa says.

"Ernest works there."

Onnie drives Ernest's truck towards Realtown, smoke puffing out the exhaust. Dust billows up and hides the Ford's tailgate. She crosses the concrete bridge and bumps over the ditch into an abandoned field where the carnival is set up. When she stops, steam spits from under the hood.

Dusky dark begs for light, but she has none. The shabbiness of the traveling show startles her. Last August, blinking lights had mesmerized her, drawing her eyes upward. Tonight, a closer look reveals most bulbs are not working. Unwashed carnies glare and blow cigarette smoke her way. She scratches the nerve rash on her hand.

Evening in Paris in Ernest's beard last night had said it all. Her eyes search for the dance tent. She heads to an oily black tent at the back where Papa said women dance naked. A quiver of music, and she quickens her stride. She breathes in spurts. To gather herself, she fingers the stiff tent flap. When she pulls it back, it creaks.

Inside, Ernest sits on a makeshift stage, cross-legged, chewing a cigar.

She offers her gift.

He does not extend his hand. "Humph." He spits.

"Don't you want it?"

He grabs her irritated hand and pulls her toward the truck. They plod through waist-high broom sedge, brittle and tan, skirting the carnival.

"Where're we going?"

"Shut up," he says. "You want ever'body to see you acting the fool?"

"There weren't no . . . " She stops. The other women. Now she knows. "The truck needs . . . " she begins.

"I said, 'Shut up.'"

Ernest parks in front of her barn. The motor puffs, hisses, and dies. Headlights cast a bleak glow through the double doors. He takes Onnie's hand, pulls her into the light, and glares at her. "You been a bad, bad girl, Onnie," he whispers.

Onnie, now trembling, nods.

Ernest takes the package and rips the paper away. The straight razor pops open with a stark click. Inside the barn, Ernest cuts a long strand of fishing line from the wall with one silent draw. The released line recoils into unraked hay.

"Lay down." He points the blade to a splotch of yellow. "Here."

Onnie kneels in the itchy hay and does not move.

"'Lay down,' I said."

Onnie breaks into a sweat, flattens out on her back and grips her hands. "What did I . . . ?"

"Shut up." Ernest wraps fishing line round her wrists and ankles. He runs a strand from stall post to stall post and binds her neck so tight that, if she tries to move, she will cut her own throat.

*Maybe I should*, she thinks. Then she won't have to face him tomorrow when the truck won't crank.

Ernest closes the doors as he leaves.

If tonight is like other August nights, Ernest sits in her kitchen, a near-empty bottle of rye whiskey before him. His dark eyes stare at red cherry clusters on her wallpaper. From time to time, he tries to rake his fingers through his long hair. It's so matted he can only push it off his forehead. Tonight, he reaches for a butcher knife and cuts clumps of hair at random. Soon he will slide down into the chair, falling out drunk.

Her papa snores, a mile away on a naked mattress.

From the floor of the horse stall, Onnie examines the sky through a hole in the roof from the last storm. One vivid star blinks. "Who's loving you?" it asks.

Shame burns on her forehead, and she snickers. This could be something special. Talking to a light. She waits for another question. There is none, so she tenders no answer.

Clouds, one a brown rabbit, another two pink piglets spotted in black, pass over the opening. Her star is gone. She scolds herself then licks salty sweat from her upper lip. "Lord have mercy, it's hot as hell." And it's dark.

Hay prickles her naked legs. Or maybe spiders, foraging for a late-night bite. Onnie shivers. The tremor ignites her rashy hand. She scratches and draws blood.

*But it'll be okay,* she thinks. *This dying. Better than this.* She breathes deep. *But there's Papa. Alone. Or Ernest. At next light.*

She rolls her eyes as far to the side as possible. An axe handle. Ernest could use the axe handle there by the door. She imagines him crushing her ankles as he whacks at the fishing line when it refuses to give. He will hand her a whittled-out crutch and say, "See, if it wasn't for me, you wouldn't be able to walk." She hears his laughter at her ear and closes her eyes.

From outside, a shaft of light slants through the roof's hole. The light drops and strikes her bosom. A brighter beam this time, stronger than the talking star. More powerful than arcing carnival spotlights.

Onnie takes another deep breath. Her eyes climb the light to the roof's opening. And up. There awaits a transformed sky. The moon is out.

"Ah. Now," she says, "this radiance, I can talk to."

# A Long Way Yet to Go

Claire Hudson double-checked her paperwork to be certain she had all the right signatures to allow her to enter the hospital. She had no idea if, when she arrived, she would be given a client or if she would be asked to select her own. If she had to select her own, what criteria would she use? Would she be expected to include what she based her decision on in her final paper?

This was her graduating semester. Spring 1966. Claire, like other social work seniors, had one final project to complete. The instructor told the class that handling this task well could be key to a strong job recommendation. The assignment required that each student must identify a dependent client, regardless of age, gender, or income. The student must learn about the individual's needs and assist in some way. The instructor sent different students to different areas of town. Claire's area bordered the western edge of Johnson's Mill Pond, which ran from the eastern edge of campus to the side of a tall, chain-link fence that encircled the Brighton Hospital compound, a long walk away.

From the time she had left her dorm room, constant arguments her mother made about not wanting Claire to be around "crazies" buzzed through her mind. She tried to shut them without success. Distracted by her uncertainties, she passed the gate. When she realized how far she had come, she stuffed her papers into her bag and went back. Two six-foot concrete obelisks held iron gates in place. She rattled the gates. The guard stepped out of his miniature house, checked her papers, and let her in.

Ancient oaks along each side of the street leading to the administration building cast dim shadows across the asphalt. At the end of the drive, a magnificent dome topped an edifice so white the building glistened. Four immense columns reached from the porch to the roof line, four-stories up. Stepped-back wings flanked the structure, three down each side. This was the most beautiful place Claire had ever seen. The complex covered acres of land. That land which wasn't housing a building lay in open furrows ready for mid-March corn and cotton plantings.

Her mind shifted back and forth from her mother's comments to her need to find ways to help people she pitied. She had been confident that helping others was her calling since she was a child. Nursing? No. She couldn't stomach blood. Teaching? She couldn't tolerate undisciplined brats. Today she was here and ready to prove her mettle.

From behind, a hand grabbed her elbow. A husky voice said, "I'm Tom."

Claire twisted and jerked her arm away. "What'd you want?"

The man, a head taller than Claire, braced his weight against a gardening hoe's handle.

"I was murdered last night, you know."

Claire couldn't breath. "No. I didn't know," she managed to say.

"Was a clown with a machete." He gripped the hoe and scraped the ground. "He offered me ice cream and when I went to take it . . . "

A man dressed in dingy white interrupted Tom's story. "Come on now, Tom," he said. He put his hand on Tom's shoulder.

Tom said, "She wants to know how I was murdered."

"I think you've told her enough. You don't want to give her nightmares." In a deliberate gait, he walked Tom away from Claire. When they were a few feet away, the orderly turned to Claire and nodded.

Up ahead, Tom was telling the guard that he had been murdered last night by a beautiful woman who tossed him out of his window . . . "

"You're on the first floor, Tom."

"Into a tub of hungry sharks and . . . "

Claire heard no more. She took a deep breath and thought again about what her mother had said. "Can't trust them crazies. Study you something else, something sensible." Claire glimpsed back the way she had come. The gates were closed, possibly locked. Patients and orderlies worked in small groups grooming the grounds. The building had so enthralled her that she missed seeing the patients. She quickened her step until she entered the double front doors and closed them behind her.

Inside, she wiped her palms down her skirt and introduced herself to the secretary. The secretary handed Claire off to a nurse dressed in stiff white from her cap to her rubber-soled oxfords. The nurse escorted Claire down a corridor painted a sickly green. Chips of old paint hung from the walls like cocoons, rolled and waiting to hatch. Claire fell behind, looking here, looking there. She passed three doors with padlocks. One door was louvered. All had a small pane of glass reinforced with wire that allowed staff to check on the patient before stepping inside. An unexpected silence crept over Claire and prickled her skin.

The nurse spoke as they passed a door that had been left ajar. "This is Benji's room. You can see he has all he needs."

Claire peeped inside. A brown metal bed frame, a mattress, a blanket that reminded Claire of Army issue for some snowy foreign country, and a plastic molded chair. No pillow. Yellow walls reflected black shadows of metal window bars over the one window. Claire wanted to step to the window to see what Benji saw when he looked outside, but the nurse had not slowed down. Claire dared not ask her to wait.

At the end of the hall, the nurse turned left. She stopped before a deep green door. "No need to worry. He's been fixed," she said.

"Fixed?"

"Fixed," the nurse repeated. She raised her hand and clicked her first two fingers together in the manner of scissors cutting. Claire blushed.

Another step and the nurse took a key from her pocket and unlocked the door. They stepped into a room foggy with sawdust. Ear-splitting hammering echoed from the far wall. The nurse walked up behind a tall man bent over a table that held two-by-fours painted an Atlantic blue-green. The man placed a short board across a longer one and hammered a four-inch nail in at the juncture. The nurse tapped his shoulder. He dropped his hammer and faced the two women.

"Claire Hudson. She's here as part of some university class," the nurse said. "Answer her questions like a good boy." She left the room and locked the door behind her.

Thick in the chest, the man towered over Claire. Sawdust covered his overalls and white muslin shirt. Claire wanted him to bend forward so she could wipe sawdust from his graying hair. Instead, she wrapped her arms around herself and rocked gently side to side.

"Well," the man said, "what'd you want?"

His hair, long on his neck and bound into a ponytail, enticed Claire to fluff out her own, to shake imaginary dust from her bob. She tilted her head. "What're you making?" she said.

41

"Crosses," he said. He picked up the hammer and two pieces of board. "For our graves."

"Whose?"

"Us. Who die here," he said. "We all die here." He paused, hammer midair. "Sooner or later." He dropped his hammer on the nail head. "A little bit day by day."

Dread kept Claire from looking him in the eye. She needed to get her project completed, so she introduced herself and extended her hand. Benji didn't respond. Her hand shook as she drew it back.

"So," she said. "Benji, one of the objectives of my assignment is to find some way to help you." She steadied her voice against its quivering.

"My name's not 'Benji.' I'm Benjamin Lloyd Hicks." He jutted his chin out as he spoke. "Outside, my friends called me 'Ben.'"

"Okay, Ben." Claire pulled up his stool and sat. "May I call you Ben?"

Again, Ben didn't acknowledge her. She took a spiral notebook and a pen from her bag and brushed sawdust from the worktable. She took a deep breath and poised her pen. "Tell me about yourself."

Ben returned to his work. "Been here since '35. Most my life." He accented each word with the hammer against the nail. "Forty-two years old last month." He slammed the hammer in a rapid succession of hits. Had Claire not seen the hammer hit the wood, she would have thought she heard gunshots. He exhaled after each stroke. "Want'a know why I'm locked up here?"

Claire wavered. "I guess so."

"Killed my grandpaw with a scythe." He glared at the wood. "I's eleven." Dents covered the slat where Ben had pounded the hammer. She shivered. She continued to hear thuds after Ben had stopped hammering.

Hesitant to ask, but with this paper due, Claire had no choice. "Why would you do that?" she murmured.

"He broke my little brother's jaws." He again punctuated each word with a slam of the hammer then dropped it to the floor. Claire jerked her foot up. "Only four years old, he was." He looked down eye to eye with Claire. "'Baby,' that's what I called him. Baby wouldn't stop crying. Grandpaw hit him in the face again and again with his fist and broke his mouth all up. He starved to death 'cause he couldn't eat. Before they buried him, my granny brought me here and left. 1935, it was."

"Your parents?" she whispered.

"Left us both when Baby was born with a club foot." Benjamin Lloyd Hicks lifted a finished cross from the table and cradled it to his chest as if it were a weeping child. "Depression and all."

"Well, Ben." Claire bit her lip as she cleared her throat. "So this is what you do all day?"

Ben picked up the handsaw and a long strip of board. He took a carpenter's scale from his back pocket and marked with a pencil where he intended to cut. "I'm a carpenter. Been a carpenter all my life. I build things." He jabbed the pencil back into his overall bib. "Crosses now." He shot Claire a glance. "Want one of my crosses?"

Claire swallowed sawdust. "I don't plan to die," she said.

"Never know what's gonna to happen. Day to day."

The room wasn't heated, yet the hair at the nape of her neck was wet. "I'm studying social work. After I graduate, I should be able to help people." Claire clicked the top of her pen in and out. Its tick-tick-tick sounded puny after the sound of Ben's hammering. "Is there some way I can help you? Something you need?"

43

Ben chuckled. He stepped so close to Claire that she could see golden dots in his dark eyes. His nose held little specks of wood. She wanted to sneeze for him. She didn't move. She mustn't be afraid. "Something you want?" she said.

"Yeah, Miss Claire Hudson." He grinned a lop-sided grin that lit up his eyes much like a little boy's. He took her hand between his large two palms. Claire noticed that his hands were whiter than her own. And soft. Too soft for a working man's hand. She resisted the urge to pull away. "I want a co-cola. A real co-cola. Brought in here so icy cold that water drips off the bottle. I want to open it myself and drink it whole." He dropped her hand. "That's what I want."

"I . . . ," she said. "I can't . . . " She stumbled, searching for words, but found none. She rose from Ben's stool. "Isn't there something else?"

"No. I just want a cold co-cola."

"Ben," she said. "I misspoke. I can't do that. You know the rules. I can't bring a bottle in here." She shifted her eyes around, surveying the space where this man spent his days. At first, she had been drawn to the emptiness, except for the worktable, his tools, and wood. Now she saw the crosses. They filled up the far corners, all in tall columns, as if each had been placed with tenderness so that it could not be scarred by another. On the wall next to her, someone had scripted "You go to Hell" in stark, red paint. Under that, in orange, someone had written "Hell's right here." She thought back to the sparse room where he spent his nights. She wasn't sure which was the reality.

She shook her head, her bob slapping her cheeks. "I can't," she said again. "I'm sorry. So sorry." She picked up her supplies and moved to the door. She tried the knob but recalled that the nurse had locked the door from the other side. Her breath came in short, quick bursts. She'd never had this much trouble breathing before. She blinked back tears. She needed to cry, but she had no idea why.

Ben materialized behind her. He took a nail and slipped it between the door and its jam. He turned the knob and opened the door.

Claire exhaled so loud she heard it herself.

"Come on back sometime, Miss Claire Hudson," he said. "I'll play you some piano. Folks say I'm right good at that." Benjamin Lloyd Hicks bent into a low, formal bow.

Claire held back a silly laugh. She straightened her back and gave him a smart salute. "Goodbye, Mr. Hicks," she said.

At first, Claire was uncertain which direction she should take to get out of the hospital. Once she turned the corner and saw the peeling paint, she knew she was headed right. While she had been in the room, lights had dimmed. The hall grew darker as she walked toward the nurses' station. Her mind told her that shouldn't be happening. She needed to go toward light, not dark. She looked at a nurse as she passed the station. The nurse tapped her long fingernails against the desk. Ragged polish did not hide the dirt under her nail tips, rather, it carried Claire's eyes to the grime. "How utterly ugly you are," Claire wanted to say. Instead, she gave a courtesy nod and walked out.

Once outside, her breath came easier. No patients. No orderlies. The grounds had been swept, bushes trimmed. The area looked more like a garden than hospital grounds.

As she approached the exit, the guard said, "Come back anytime." He closed the gate behind her. Evening quiet amplified a metallic click, and something inside Claire stored the sound. The finality of the lock told her she would not return.

In the distance, the sun cast a hazy light over fields. A deep darkness would overtake her before she made it home.

# Letter from Vicksburg, 1863

May 20

Dearest M,

I dare not use your name lest you be associated with my time here. Please destroy this correspondence as soon as you read it.

As you know, Capt. H brought me to stay with our Auntie V before Sherman overran Jackson and blocked our return to Mobile, as I had promised, by destroying the rails. Yankees have held Vicksburg under siege since May 18.

When I arrived by rail May 5, I refused to leave Auntie's home. It was not until a cannon ball uprooted a camellia that shaded the south veranda yesterday during heavy shelling that I recognized our true danger. I was sitting in that shade, Dear M, when dirt showered down on me like rain. At that point, Auntie and I ran down the bluff on which her house sits. I had to drag my slave J with me all the way. She is such a simpleton.

We moved into the cave that Auntie had her manservant cut into clay before he disappeared. It was just before the cannon hit that we learned Grant had moved south from Memphis and Farragut had blockaded New Orleans and sent vessels north.

My residence is quite primitive as I am forced to live the life of a backwoodsman with only a bed and chair for comfort. J cooks our food on an open fire at the entrance. With what little money I have, I send her up the bluff and into market when shelling is light. She cries and begs to remain with me in the cave. "Them guns, they scares me, Mz R," she says. I tell her to get up off the floor, and I send her on her way. I must eat.

46

## May 23

The earth here is unlike any I have known. It looks like white clay. It is soft, but hard at the same time. It cuts easy as butter. If it is cut perpendicular, it stands strong as a wall and holds its shape, so unlike Alabama riverbank clay. Cut it on an angle, and it crumbles. Locals call it loess.

Before I arrived, multiple caves had been carved into these bluffs for shelter against the Yankees. Each cave is one or two rooms with an opening facing the Mississippi. From the western banks, the bluffs must look like gigantic honeycombs. Shellings and shootings have been constant since we moved underground, but it rarely reaches us here.

## June 6

Auntie V is dead. She died from dysentery. I laid her near the back wall, for J refused to go in and out the entrance if she could see Auntie. "Don't make me go past no dead body," J begged. No amount of beating would make her go foraging, which she must do now, for my resources are gone and there is little left to buy. The burial brigade called from above the next morning, and I answered with "Female body. One." I know not where she was taken.

How lonely here with only myself and J.

## June 17

It was after the moon rose that the soldier came. He had crawled to the entrance, but he could not make it over the ledge J had cut to block heavy rain. J found him before the sun rose. She ran into the back room where we store what food and water she manages to gather. I have my bed there so she cannot steal what I have. She awakened me, jabbering about a dead man. She hopped up and down, pointing toward the entrance, her eyes as round as a cow's.

He still lived. We dragged him across the threshold, clay crumbling beneath his weight.

The soldier, a Yankee, would tell me between gasps that ruffians found him on the outskirts of town and beat him with axe handles. They threw him over my bluff for dead. Perhaps they thought he would sink in the Mississippi as it has been high several times since I arrived.

I pulled him and J pushed. We laid him in my bed to hide him from the cave's opening. I sent J to Auntie's house for petticoats to use as bandages. We have no sulfur or lard to make salves, but J took some of the wood she had stowed and traded it among her people for healing herbs.

He moans days and cries out at night. The leg festers and swells. I have to bring out the leather strap to make J cleanse his wounds. His body is battered, but his most serious injury is his lower calf where bone sticks through skin three inches or more. All we can do is wrap the leg to keep away flies.

June 19

He does not improve and is often delirious. The wound is shades of purples, greens, and, in places, black. The stench of rot fills both rooms of the cave.

I doubt he will survive the leg.

June 21

How I have tossed about my choices, Dearest M.

Yankees come from all directions. Our soldiers have been crossing from the western bank at night to visit family or, I am ashamed to write these despicable words, to desert. I hope each night that Capt. H will come, but he has not. If he does come, what will I do? When I am discovered, how will I explain a Yankee in my bed when Capt. H has spent these last 35 days of siege defending his Confederacy? Defending me, his wife?

June 24

J ran away last night. I am alone with the Yankee. I sent her yesterday to find meat. She returned carrying a fat skinned gopher tied to an oak limb. This is all that remains. Two weeks ago, I refused for four days to eat soup made from bark and a dog skeleton she had scavenged.

I understand why she ran. I would run myself, but I have no place to go. And I have the soldier.

J will not survive unless she meets some of her kind beyond the embankments surrounding Vicksburg, for she knows nothing that is true and lacks direction unless I tell her what to do.

You recollect her. Capt. H bought her across the river from Tuscaloosa before she could walk. She and her mother who was bought to cook for us. Her mother jumped to her death from our barn loft while she was heavy with her next child. It died. Capt. H said, "No matter. Just another slave." I was surprised at his lack of concern, for he places high value on his house slaves, but I digress.

It has fallen to me to feed and bath him. His body differs so from Capt. H, who is fair. He has much coarser hair and it covers his entire body. While here, he has grown a beard that tints red when I hold the candle near. But his blood dries the same color as Capt. H's when he cuts his cheek shaving. I call him Isaac.

June 25

Isaac worsens. I groped my way up the bluff last night while there was a new moon. I took an axe Auntie had hidden under the woodpile and brought back as many logs as I could carry. Coming down, I slipped and dropped several, but I believe I have enough for a fire to cleanse the axe. I have heard stories that one can chop off a leg at the knee. If the leg is tightly bound at the hip, the patient will not bleed to death. The only thing left to do is sear the wound. I go now to build a hot fire.

June 26

I could not do it, Dearest M. I lifted the axe over my head and aimed at the putrid leg.

As I was about to drop the weapon with all my strength garnered toward that point, the boy opened his grey eyes and whispered, "I cannot live without my leg."

He knew!

How like a monster I must have seemed. Perhaps he saw only the raised axe. I do not know. The agony in those young eyes forced me to sway. He closed his eyes and waited. Yes. He knew.

I clinched my teeth and slammed the axe blade into his face.

June 28

Last night late, I whittled out bloodstained clay from

the walls and ground it into the floor. I managed to roll the boy over the bluff, and I burned the bloodied bedding. The cave is hot as Hades.

June 30

I received word from a group of stragglers. More of our soldiers are flooding the city this morning. Capt. H crossed the Mississippi under cover of darkness last evening. He should be here mid-day.

Your loyal and devoted Cousin,
RH

*Lt. Gen. John C. Pemberton, CSA surrendered his remaining 30,000 troops at Vicksburg, MS to Maj. Gen. Ulysses S. Grant, USA July 4, 1863. The City of Vicksburg would not celebrate the Fourth of July again until 1943.*

## Motherhood

"My mother had a great deal of trouble with me, but I think she enjoyed it." - Mark Twain

# That Which Passes

Drained by early pregnancy and its intermittent nausea, Ellen allows herself to slide back into sleep after Dick and Ricky leave for t-ball practice. It is Saturday and she can rest.

At 10:17, the phone rings. She jerks upright. A twinge tugs against her lower back. She circles her hand over her stomach and arches out her belly in anticipation of months to come.

Coach Corley. Weather is what she hears. Dick's not back. Can she pick Ricky up, or should he take the boy home with him? Storm's moving in fast.

Had this call come earlier in her marriage, she would have folded accordion-like, her voice tightened into off-key screeches. Things change. These four years, she has watched Ricky grow from babyhood into a child who idolizes his father, and she shelters the both of them. Now this.

In the bathroom, she grabs the counter to steady her head. The reality of Dick leaving their son so he can sneak off with Abby Summerfield has her body no longer grounded, her head light. Knowing where Dick is draws her soul out of its body and carries it upward. Were she to close her eyes, she would rise, oblivious, leaving her body clumped below.

In the kitchen, she shoves Dick's coffee cup and Ricky's half-eaten toast aside. They left in a rush. Ellen wonders how little time passes on mornings when Dick strokes her back, loving her, then showers and moves on to his lover. She pulls out a bag of artificially flavored popcorn and tosses it into the microwave. Punching in three minutes, she knows this baby does not need fake stuff. She does. She needs something on her stomach.

*No*, she thinks, *this mess calls for hard liquor.* But that won't work either. She has another child to think about. At least she won't have to explain to the coach. She picks up the puffed paper bag and tears it open to release the steam.

The phone rings again. Caller ID lights up Abby Summerfield's name. "It's Dick," she says. "His stomach. Hemorrhaging." In town this size, she knows not to call an ambulance.

Sweat dampens Ellen's face. Consumed by anger and queasiness, she breathes hard thinking, *Dear Lord, let this pass.* She stomps her foot to clear her head and starts to hang up. "Damn you, Dick Parker," she says aloud.

Static from the rising storm shoots through the phone.

"Mrs. Parker?" Abby speaks. "Are you there?"

Ellen needs to hang up. She needs to get her son before the storm breaks. After a moment, she asks, "Dick know you called?"

"No." Abby answers so quietly Ellen strains to hear.

"Why not?" It's a rhetorical question. Some things remain true about Dick. Not damaging his public image is one.

Outside the house, Ellen senses the day is bad. Gummy air reveals severe storms close at hand. To the east, dense black clouds filter air into faded green, almost yellow, tornado weather. Raised in the south, she knows storms rising from the east. They can be killers.

She picks up lunch for Ricky and heads for the t-ball field. Ricky tears into his fries and chocolate milk. Before they reach the main road into town, greasy smells from the kiddy burger meal and butter-flavored popcorn saturate her hair, coat her skin. She feels slimy. Watching Ricky in the rearview mirror, sometimes baby, sometimes child, she hopes he'll be asleep soon. The less he knows the better.

The storm pops up out of nowhere, as April storms tend to do in central Alabama. Wind whistles through the upper air. Sycamore leaves turn from green to silver as wind twists their underside to face the on-coming storm. Ellen fights the gusts, thinking she has a flat or she has lost control of the car. Or of herself.

Her dignity rises with uncertain questions: should she go to Dick or leave the two on their own? Abby Summerfield is a college co-ed, she has decided. Probably a bouncy one with long blonde hair. Panic in her phone call told Ellen she has no experience handling a man who vomits blood after eating strong Mexican spices.

Craving salt, Ellen digs into the popcorn. Her window down, she expects fresh air to smother the nausea that rises in her throat. A sudden drop in air pressure pushes heavy on her chest. Pregnancy heaves run chilling shivers down her arms.

She glances in the rearview mirror and combs buttery fingers through her tawny hair. While brushing her hair this morning, she recognized her coloring isn't the pale she had with Ricky during her first two months. Today's pasty complexion is more leftover raw potato. Maybe she'll call the OBGYN Monday to get her blood count checked. She fans a hand across her face to stir the humidity, but the humidity has settled, mashing its dampness into every living thing. It will not release its hold until after the storm. She closes the window and turns on the air-conditioner.

Tenth Street and Azalea Avenue. The intersection appears out of nowhere. Ellen flips on the blinker and turns onto Tenth. She revs the Buick's motor, headed toward student apartments across from Forest Glen Cemetery. Once she makes the turn, she relaxes. Her decision has come to her without thought. She is Mrs. Dick Parker and she has come to reclaim her husband.

At Tenth Street, Ellen parks across from Abby Summerfield's apartment. When Ellen opens the back car door, Ricky sets his milk on the floorboard, ready to follow.

"Stay here, Sweetheart. Mommy will be right back. I just need a hug."

"I wanna go." He starts to climb out. "Daddy didn't come back," he whines. "Coach had to wait for you. He got mad." He puffs his lips.

"Coach is not mad at you." She reassures him she will be back and hands him his book *Where the Wild Things Are.* "Read the pictures."

"I know this one." He pushes the book toward her.

She shoves it back, harder than she had meant. "Read it anyway. I'll be right back."

Ricky picks up his plastic milk bottle and sits down. She kisses his forehead and closes the door.

Ellen crosses the street at a jog. Dogwood petals torn loose by the approaching storm fall round her like paper snippets dropped from the sky. Ellen loves dogwood blooms, their four white petals, according to legend, tipped with a spot of sacrificial blood. They are whiter against dark clouds, these dogwood blooms. In comes a storm and strips trees naked. Just when they are at their best.

Ellen knew where to come. Since moving outside Tuscaloosa a year ago, she memorized Abby Summerfield's address from letters she found when packing for the move from Montgomery, letters Dick had collected over the last four years and hidden in a box inside his closet. The first time Ellen saw the Tuscaloosa address, Dick's business trips and his willingness to move north weakened a major tie within her, a tie she once thought never could be loosened.

The afternoon she first discovered the letters, Ricky had cried from where he napped in the next room. She went to him that day and returned each day to the closet to read the letters, one by one, while her son slept. The words flooded her body, taking her breath away, sometimes almost drowning her when she read a love phrase that he so often spoke to her. In their marriage bed. In their little house. With their son sleeping close by. By the time she had read all the letters, shock had moved into numbness. It bowed her shoulders with an overwhelming weight that rides there still.

Reading the printed words brought the realization that this lie, this stowing of the letters, betrayed her as much as did his infidelity, simply because he buried them inside their home. It was as if he brought this woman into their bedroom and allowed her to watch as they slept.

Rusted iron railing runs half the length of the fla-mingo-colored stucco building, separating the sidewalk from cinder block steps leading to the basement door. Standing on the top step, she braces her hand against the rough wall then sits, knees weak. The building shelters her from the wind. She waits to gather her breath.

In the car across the street, Ricky waits. She questions her decision to leave him alone. Spring storms out of the east are dangerous. First, an air so electrically changed it mashes your breath back into your chest, stark lightning, then boisterous thunder, followed by rain so dense it seems more fog than water. Locals mark historical years by freak snowstorms blown in on arctic air, snows from light smatterings that weaken stalks and leaves blooms drooping, to heavy cover, dropping limbs across power lines, swaying and breaking, enclosing entire towns in black. Left behind is the cold grief of heady blood-red tulips, stark against dingy snow.

Ellen rises. Her senses elevated, she notices every movement her body makes. She counts each step to the landing. At the bottom, she stops. "What the hell am I doing here?" she asks. "Let him lie there and die."

A gust of wind blows dogwood blossoms off the sidewalk, down the stairwell. She read once that a dogwood bloom is not a bloom at all, but a cluster of green buds surrounded by four white leaves that look like petals. White leaves drop. Center berries fill out into tiny red fruit that perpetuates the life of the tree. She does not like the idea of four white leaves. She wants each be an entity, one bloom complete, with its consistent pattern of white and a splotch of red.

A leaf cluster or petal or whatever-it-is, its tips near-black with redness, totters on the edge of the step above her. One petal torn away by its upheaval, only three remain. The incomplete cluster drops down the stairway and settles at her foot. Nothing is ever what it seems.

Ellen takes a deep breath and knocks.

Abby Summerfield opens the door as if she'd been waiting on the other side. Petite and stocky, she is older than Ellen by at least ten years, in her late thirties, early forties maybe. Age shows in her slender throat, wrinkled like a wild turkey's. Brown hair hits her chin when she moves her head. If she has an upper lip at all, it curls back into her mouth, invisible.

Dick once said he liked Ellen's full lips. He lied.

"I'm Abby," the woman says, lifting her hand slightly as if offering a welcome.

Ellen looks at the hand and ignores it. "Where's my husband?"

"In there." She tips her head toward an arch at the top of the steps behind her.

Neither moves.

"I'll tell him you're here."

"No. I'll tell him," Ellen replies, her jaw tight.

"This is still my house, Mrs. Parker." Abby stiffens.

"Yes. Your house. My husband, Ms. Summerfield."

Abby Summerfield turns and goes up the three steps to the bedroom.

Ellen steps inside the apartment. She is blinded for a moment by darkness. There are no windows. Behind her, wind sucks the door and it slams, locking her into the square room.

A copper pyramid shade hangs low over a slick yellow Formica table that separates the strip kitchen from the rest of the room. No open peanut butter jars, no stained coffee mugs or empty cereal boxes, not even a crumpled paper towel clutter the counter top.

On the table, a hodge-podge of jig-saw pieces face toward two metal folding chairs, side by side. Ellen recognizes an Escher, Dick's favorite. Stairways that lead nowhere then convolute onto themselves. Lizards following lizards following lizards' tails. Everything moving without going anywhere, everything turning in on itself. At home, Dick works the puzzles alone. Their spiraling pattern makes her dizzy.

She stares at the puzzle. "My God," she whispers. "Dick's at home here." The concept unnerves her, and her left breast responds, throbbing as if milk-full, as if Ricky is an infant again and needs to suckle, as if the forming child has already begun his own demands. She drops her keys, instinctively covers the breast with her hand, then forsakes it and grips her left wrist.

Before her, angular light throws severe shadows across the room. White ceramic angels, so white they look soft, some tall, others short, sit clustered on the sofa table. One pillow, a shaped needlepoint angel with stiff gold wings and metallic halo, leaves no room for sitting in an overstuffed navy chair. A cluster of wooden angels painted in Renaissance reds and blues stands on the bottom step leading to the arched access to the bedroom, as if guarding the entrance. Another, dressed in rose chiffon, topped with a tinsel halo and what looks like white chicken feathers for wings, hangs by fishing line from the ceiling. Navy carpet speckled with gray dots reverses Ellen's perspective and displaces her. She floats in a dark sky, in an upside-down world. She lifts her head toward the angel wobbling back and forth above her and gulps back tears.

Abby Summerfield appears at the top of the landing. "I collect," she says.

Ellen bites her lower lip.

Abby moves down a step and stops by a plywood angel propped against the wall. Washed, rather than painted, with blues and golds to make it appear old and valuable, it stands almost three feet tall.

Aware of the angel's size, Ellen remembers Ricky, alone in the car, and thinks she needs to see about him. "I need to make this quick," she says.

Abby steps into the living room to let Ellen pass, then, as if she thinks of something, she edges back, blocking Ellen from the bedroom entrance, and extends her hand.

"Don't touch me." Ellen outstretches her arms, palms held up flat toward this woman. If she touches Abby Summerfield's skin, it will be scaly, like a rat's tail.

62

"He makes me happy," Abby says.

Ellen glares. "Sounds like the same spiel he gives me." She steps past Abby Summerfield, up into the bedroom. "Almost every night," she adds, the words blowing away as if caught by the outside wind.

Dingy light strains through transom glass across the top of the room. A mattress on box springs rests on the floor, flush against an underground brick wall. The open window funnels the wind's whistle down the outside stairwell, followed by close rumbling thunder. Ellen glances up toward the street. If she stands on tiptoe, she can see her Buick's tires.

Dick lies under a muslin comforter covered with over-sized purple pansies. Ellen glowers at her husband. "Couldn't you at least have pulled off your wedding band?"

"Don't start, Ellen," Dick says.

"So. This is why we moved to Tuscaloosa." Thunder moves closer. Or perhaps a transfer truck passes on the highway going south.

"What time is it? Where's Ricky?"

"Outside. In the car."

"You brought him here?" Dried black blood cracks on his lips when he speaks.

"What did you want me to do? Leave him by himself at the ballpark?"

Dick looks away from her. "I need help." He balls his fist and grinds it above his navel, swallowing when he speaks, drinking his own spit. A yellow towel fills a green plastic bowl by the bed. Water, past red but not yet black, borders the towel. This much blood has not been part of the attacks before.

"Get up," Ellen demands.

He shifts his legs. "I didn't mean for this to happen."

"What? Get caught? Or have an affair for five years?"

"It's not been…" He lifts himself up on his elbow.

"Don't lie, Dick. I've known about her for over a year," Ellen stares at him. "If you didn't want me to know, why bother to call me?"

"She should not have." Splats of rain ricochet off the transom windows where they stick out toward the sidewalk. "This is not what I wanted. I thought I could go home." He pulls the cover over his nakedness. "Ricky can't know. He'll remember and never understand," Dick whispers.

"Oh, and I will?" she asks. It is as if she has stumbled on an intimate moment Dick should have kept to himself. She turns her back on him.

"You're always there for me. All these years." Dick gulps behind her. "I've always been there for you." Lowering his voice, he tries to soften her with an impersonation of her father the night he caught them naked in the back seat of Dick's car. Her dad beating his fist against the car window while Ellen tugged at her skirt and Dick tried to pull up his Levis. The neighbor's light coming on to see what was happening. An incident they still laugh about.

"But I didn't marry you because he said I had to. You know that." He stretches out his hand again.

Ellen says nothing.

"Don't make me beg, Ellen. You're my wife." He sounds like Ricky whining for another dish of ice cream.

"I'm more aware of that than you, obviously." Ellen speaks to the wall.

A car passes down the street overhead, its tires splattering light rain like water on hot bacon grease. Suddenly exhausted, Ellen's rising fullness overwhelms her, draining her face. Earth's force magnifies itself and, from within her body, pulls her arms and legs disproportionately out of shape so she can't connect what's happening in the room with what's inside her head. She presses her hand against the brick for support and blinks, rather than let him see her cry.

"Sit up and put your pants on. I'll take you to the hospital." With effort, she tugs at the comforter. Dick pulls back. She turns from him again. "That's all I promise." Another moment of staring at the raw brick wall and she speaks, "I'm having a baby."

"You're what?"

"I'm pregnant. Early December." When she faces him, she cannot read the emptiness in his face. "A Christmas gift, you might say."

"Take me home." He speaks so quietly she turns her ear to hear. His voice rises when Ellen does nothing. "Do something, woman. God, I'm your husband. I'm ready to go home. It's my right."

His anger, like dirty dishwater tossed carelessly into the yard, soils her. She looks away from the transom to see what dimmed the room, if more clouds have closed in, or if someone turned off the light. Nothing names the change.

She stalks forward. His usual rages have him standing over her. This time positions reverse. She, not Dick, speaks. "Your right? You think I have to take you in? You saying I owe you?" She lowers her voice. "Why?"

Dick cowers further under the comforter.

"Because I birthed your son?"

Ellen leans over the bed, directly into his face, surprising herself with her quietness. "You're wrong, Dick Parker. Going home has nothing to do with me having to take you in. You go home, not because I have to let you. You go home only if I want you to."

Her voice lowers to a scratchy whisper. "You go home because Ricky needs you more than that woman does. I won't have her raise my son. And she can't have you simply because she's not got a man of her own."

She takes a breath. "You go home only when I decide you're fit to be around our son."

Suddenly out of breath, she sits down on the bed near Dick's feet. Realizing she is on the bed where they lie, she bursts back up. "Besides, this baby needs a father. Be it you or not." A blast of wind blows dogwood petals against the wet windows. One sticks, flattened like a lopsided cross against the transom.

For the first time, Ellen genuinely doubts her logic in getting pregnant. That night Dick pulled his face out of her hair and hovered above her. His arms, braced on the sheet, shimmered bronze like Monarch wings in candle-light. In the shadow, the young man she married ten years before smiled down at her and whispered "I love you, Ellen." And she thought, this is my husband. Out of his loins came my son, my sweet son. She opened herself to him, broad like a squash blossom, yellow and warmed by mid-day heat. When she woke the next morning, she knew she was pregnant.

Throughout her life, Ellen Parker has invested in the idea that whatever pleasure she knows comes to her through a hard wall of pain. The fire in her legs from Dick's touch after his first thrust, joy in her marriage after the humiliation of her father finding them half-naked in the car, and Ricky, her Ricky, after the sweat, the splintering, the ripping of birthing him. Now the daily waking walking hellfire of Abby Summerfield. Like some primitive National Geographic warrior who trods barefoot over hot coals in anticipation of a promised feast, she will make it through. She has no choice.

"Where's Ricky?" Dick puts a hand over his groin and pulls the comforter closer with the other.

"I told you. Come. Get up."

"He know where you are?" He rolls over on his side.

"Get up, I said." Ellen pulls his head off the pillow with one arm and drags his legs off the mattress with the other. Her baby doesn't need this.

An imprint of Dick's head remains in the pillow.

"We're going to the hospital." She lowers her shoulders to lift him off the bed.

"Ellen?" Dick drapes an arm around her neck.

"Shut up, Dick." Her words come out through clinched teeth.

The mattress sits so low that, with his sock feet on the floor, Dick's knees stick up in the air like broken marionette legs. Ellen bends down and tugs his socks up from where they have wadded around his ankles. Same old Dick. Always wears his socks to bed.

Sliding her arms under his armpits to lift him, Ellen inhales the stale oniony odor of their morning sex. She stifles a heave, then swallows, refusing either of them the satisfaction of her vomit on their bold-faced pansies.

As she boosts him up off the mattress, Dick presses his face into her neck. His cheeks damp, she wonders if he's sweating or crying or both.

"I do love you." He speaks into her neck. "You have to believe me."

Ellen pulls at dead weight. "Stand up. I can't do this by myself."

"I'm trying." He collapses back on the mattress and gasps for breath.

She picks his khakis up off the floor and slips them over his feet.

"My shorts. I can't go without my shorts."

Ignoring him, she works the pants up over his knees, then his hips, and tries to lift him again. He tumbles back on the mattress, the slacks gaping open below his navel. His body looks older somehow than when he left this morning.

Unable to move him, Ellen goes to the living room.

Sitting on the bottom step of the landing, Abby palms her forehead.

"Call an ambulance."

"He doesn't . . . " Abby starts.

"Do it anyway." Walking toward the door, "I'm going to see about my son," she says.

Ricky sleeps, one sock on, one sock off. His hair, shoe polish brown like Dick's, sticks to his forehead. Asleep, he is so much like Dick that she wants to shake him. Rain no more than sprinkles and a lull in the wind fool her into a false sense of change, until a sideways wind gust yanks her hair away from her head as if trying to drag her down the street. She kisses her fingertips and places them on Ricky's head, against where his infant's soft spot had been, where she's felt his warm pulse so many times before.

Back inside, Ellen drops cross-legged on the floor at the bed's foot. Staring at the blank wall, she listens to Dick breathe in and out on the mattress above her. In the quiet, the room now dark from lowered clouds, she waits. A hollowness inside her yearns for something, she cannot know what. Perhaps a heavy swell of rain to break and begin the onslaught. Something to let the rain make the storm official.

An empty beer bottle rolls under the iron railing, over the transom ledge, and shatters on the linoleum floor.

Dick lifts his head. "What's that?"

"Storm," Ellen answers. "Lie back down."

Rising from the floor, she pulls herself up by the mattress edge. "I'm going outside to Ricky. I don't want him to wake up and be scared by the weather."

"Don't go."

"I'm going, Dick." She sighs. "Your . . . she's called the ambulance. Ricky and I'll meet you at the hospital." Weakness turns to weariness. "See that she's not there." Without turning back, she walks past Abby Summerfield, leaving the door open behind her.

Outside, early afternoon is as dark as late evening. The street is empty. From inside the car, Ricky's face makes a tiny circle, a stark white balloon set on a flimsy stick and glued to the back window.

Ellen runs against stiff wind, grappling in her pocket for keys. Not there. She must have left them in the car.

The ground is now clear of dogwood blooms. Another season gone.

She opens the door to Ricky's reprimand. "Mommy, you left me."

"No, Baby, I'm here," she calls over whipping wind. She hears someone running toward her and looks around for help. But no one's there. Instead, a black limb somersaults down the street in her direction.

Ellen grabs him out of the car. Knife-slicing pain cuts across her back, encircling her belly as she lifts the child. Folding double, Ellen squeezes out the cramp. Blood rushes out of her face and gushes down her thighs, leaving her faint.

"Oh, God, no," she cries. "Not my baby."

Lightning breaches the sky as rain the color of unbleached bed sheets advances down the street. Somewhere a siren blasts. An ambulance? A tornado warning? Ellen can't know which is which.

Lifting Ricky up on her hip, she hoists him around the waist like a sack of flour and tosses him into the front seat. No keys.

"I left my keys, sweetheart. I'll be right back." Ellen slams the car door and runs. Her wet hair wound into tendrils slaps her face.

Inside she searches the dimness, her eyes darting back and forth. Abby still sits on the step next to her angel.

"Keys?"

Abby flips on the overhead light.

Ellen grabs the keys off the puzzle, its pieces scattering over the floor. Outside a pop resounds as if a bone has broken. Ellen knows the sound. One of the cemetery's old oaks has split. Snapped.

She dashes for the door and battles her way up, into leaves and limbs, fighting her way to the top. Before she reaches the highest step, she can see the car where she left Ricky.

There is no street. Only a thick oak limb broken away to expose the old tree's hollow core. It rests in a swag cut in the Buick's trunk, slicing through, smashing the car, like an empty aluminum can.

Ellen runs, screaming, toward the car.

Out of the branches comes a tiny voice calling for his mommy.

# Moon Shadows Dancing

Jacob laid the flattened brown bear on the pillow next to Lillie. Here, Mother. Here's your bear. It's after midnight. Now go back to sleep.

I want your wife to come here.

Myrna's at her mother's this week. Her mama's sick. This is Myrna's week to stay. It's just you and me tonight.

A full moon brought heavy oak limbs into the room. Lillie watched as they set black across the wall.

Tell Winston to come to bed.

Dad's not here, Mother. He's gone.

Dancing, Lillie said.

No, Mother. Dad's dead. Twelve years now. Hold your bear and go to sleep.

She put her hand on the bear and looked at her fingers in the twilight from her night light. Seventy-one years of holding on to things showed in the knuckles. Gnarls turned them inward so she couldn't grasp the fur. Lillie rubbed her palm across the bear's chest.

She ran her fingers up through Winston's chest hair. At fourteen, a new bride, Lillie's never felt a man's chest hair before. Prickly, like the hair between her legs. It surprised her, snagging her fingers in the tangles.

Winston? Lillie rubbed his face with her hand and talked with her eyes closed. Remember the summer Paw worked in Knoxville? Maw danced with moon shadows. On the front porch.

Winston pulled up her gown and settled himself over her. That's just your imagining, Lillie. Shadows don't dance. The belch of his beer as he kissed her tasted bitter. He smelled like sun-rotted fruit.

71

No, Winston. Lillie turned her face away. She knew what she was talking about. I stood in the door to the dog-trot and watched her. Who's that dancing on the porch with you, Maw? I said. Go back to sleep, Lillie girl, Maw said. She took my hand, her hand sticky with juice, and walked me back in, all shimmery with her nightgown wrapping round her legs. Smelling like oranges saved over from Christmas. Did Paw bring us oranges, Maw? I said. Who brought you an orange? Can I eat oranges with you, Maw? A laugh moved in from the corner of the porch. Who's that man, Maw? Nobody. Just the breeze, Lillie. Go back to sleep. It's late. Little girls just turned six, they need their sleep, Maw said. But moon shadows come back, Winston. They come back all summer long.

Hush, Lillie, Winston said.

Lillie edged her hips up to meet his. Winston. His weight nestled her into the mattress. Winston.

Don't talk, Lillie, Winston whispered, and he laid his hand over her mouth. Just lay still. I'll tell you when to move.

Lillie opened her eyes and watched the tree limbs climb across the ceiling. The cornshuck mattress rattled like Winston's knees were bothering something buried inside. Winston kissed her forehead and rolled back onto the bed.

Here's a good night kiss, Mother. Now stay in bed this time. I'll turn the lamp on for you.

Jacob talked under water when he moved in the dark. He closed Lillie's bedroom door.

My lamp's flickering, Jacob, Lillie said.

Jake, your mother's up again. The voice drifted under water. Not Myrna. Myrna's voice floated. On top of the water, like leaves fresh off a tree.

Be quiet. Just be still. I'll see what she wants.

72

Jacob opened the door. Not thirty minutes and you're up again, Mother. Jacob unscrewed the light bulb and gave it to Lillie.

There's three different elephants in a single bulb, Jacob said. When the light flickers, one's gone for good.

Elephants. I don't see no elephants. Lillie turned the spent bulb in her hand. She couldn't see inside.

Elements, Mother. Elements. When the elements go out, the light won't burn.

Somebody painted this damn thing white. I don't see no need for such. Nothing wrong with a good lamp where you can wash out the globe and turn down the wick when the moon comes up.

The light's okay now. Don't cuss. It's not like you. And don't get back up, Mother. I need to get some sleep.

The moon's come up, Jacob.

Yes, Mother I know.

Jacob's voice had turned old, like Winston's.

I want your wife to come here.

No, Mother. No. I told you. Myrna's not here.

Jacob turned out the night light and closed Lillie's door.


Jacob had moved Lillie into town last year. Into the same house in Copeland's Crossing where he brought Myrna where they married twenty-six years before. Into a room next to the tree so there'd be night shadows on the wall.

You'll like it here, Myrna had said. You can't keep staying out there in that house by yourself. The nearest farm's at least a mile down the road. What if something happened to you?

This is the best room in the house, Mother. Just look at this live oak. It's at least as old as the front yard oak on the farm. You can watch the seasons change, Jacob'd said. And you can leave the window open for the breeze. It'll be just like sleeping outside.

They's rats dancing on the ceiling, Jacob.

Good Lord, Jake. Is she still up? We should've gone to my place.

Hush, Angie. I have to be here when Myrna's gone. You know that. No, Mother. No rats. It's acorns rolling down the roof. Acorns off the tree.

Jacob's voice sounded deeper when he was in the next room.

It's raining in here, son. Ain't it raining in there where you are? I can hear creaking. Is the wind rising?

No, Mother. There's no wind. Go to sleep.


The second summer, the second summer after Maw's passing, a summer of rain after rain, rain pressing steam up and out of the land; a summer of fever taking child after child, Lillie and Winston laid the dead baby out in a dresser drawer while neighbors nailed the coffin in the back yard. Lillie put the coffin in the kitchen where her cot had stood the summer she was six. The summer when Maw danced on the porch. Balanced it on two chairs with split oak bottoms.

The night the baby died, Lillie called Winston in. Go to the corn crib and bring me some shuck, she said.

Shuck for what? Winston asked.

A mattress. I'm making my baby a mattress. For the coffin. She can't lay flat on the bottom of a hard wood box.

Don't be a fool, Lillie. Nobody puts a mattress in a coffin. If you want shuck, go get it yourself.

Stay out of the corn crib, Lillie, Maw said. They's rats in there.

74

You're a damn fool. Folks'll think you're crazy, woman.

Bring me some shuck, Winston.

Rats big enough to carry a little girl off, Maw said. Stay out of that corn crib, child.

Just bring me some shuck, please, Winston. That's all I'm asking. For my baby.

I'll bring you shuck, woman. I'll bring a bushel of shuck to shut you up.

Lillie cut the muslin and threaded her needle. She built a fire against rats that come with the night and stitched by the shadows as fire danced over logs. Summer or no, fire'd keep rats away from shuck. Finished, she laid her child on the mattress. The fire popped and spit at the crackles of shuck laid on shuck as Lillie settled the body.

A neighbor come with a box camera. Bad to lose a first child, the neighbor said.

They're young. They can have more, another said. This won't matter after a time.

The camera made Lillie a likeness of the baby lying still, like the concrete angel atop a small headstone, its feet naked, pointing straight up. The picture was lost but it had stayed in Lillie's head. Brought in by the moon and rats dancing in shadows on the ceiling.

Winston had folded up on the ground and cried when the men set the little box in for burial. He walked the yard the whole of the wake and hadn't looked once at the child.

Lillie sat by the box throughout the night and stared at the fire moving back and forth in the fireplace grate. The whole summer following, she slept days and stayed awake nights, holding the rats at bay.

I sleep better when the room's green, Lillie told Myrna.

The room is clean, Lillie. I just cleaned it myself.

Jacob's wife Myrna, she's a good wife. You've got a good wife, Jacob. She keeps the shade down on the street side window.

To keep the street out, Myrna said.

To keep Lillie in, Jacob said.

Hush, Jacob. Your mother'll hear you.

When the air sits untroubled, Lillie longs to float out the window to walk the leaves of the old oak tree turned summer green. She keeps the side window open so the sun's rise can drive out moon shadows, mixing its light with light off the leaves. Sunlight waltzes in, silent, so Lillie can sleep through the day. Then darkness and shoes of shadows dancing wake her, to talk to Jacob.

The world, warm with the touch of re-creation, spread itself open for Lillie the summer before Winston brought Jacob home. Alone, hot nights with Winston working the next farm over, Lillie would climb up the front yard oak to a broad plank shelf Paw made for her when she was ten. A wife these fifteen years, her husband gone away to work, she'd sleep easy with night shadows stroking her body, cool, like lullabies.

Maw died the spring Lillie and Winston married. Ten years had passed since Maw left them the dogtrot house, the sixty acres, and words penciled on lined paper folded and stuck in the family Bible. Ten years gone, Winston working somebody else's farm, Lillie, asleep in the tree one night in early summer, watched Maw come back and sway on the porch. Lillie squeezed her eyes shut so's not to see. Eyes closed against the vision, Lillie lived the past and dreamed

76

the present; she never knew she held the difference in the back of her mind.

Lillie dreamed Maw's last porch dance a summer night just months before Jacob came home with his father. Maw danced in the moonlight, in time with deep laughter, 'til Lillie saw Winston move out of the night. From under the trees, Winston stepped on the porch. He nodded to Maw, now a shade on the wall, so dim that she blended with grim, empty shadows. Maw merged with the darkness and vanished. Winston turned, bowed, then offered his hand to the woman who had shadowed him from behind the corn crib.

Lillie lay in her tree while she stood in the door of the dogtrot. Both wife and child, she watched Winston move slow, slow as Maw, float out under the trees, night after night, with shadows in nightgowns aglimmer, nightgowns short, nightgowns loose.

Winston started his dance, and Maw left the porch. Nights without moons Lillie knew when Winston was back, returned from his dance, proclaimed by the smell of split oranges when he stepped on the porch.

Steps woke Lillie. A man and a woman laughing small laughs. There on Jacob's side of the house. Creaks from his room next door. Lillie opened her eyes.

Moon shadows spilled into the room, whirling, spinning, over the facing wall, reeling faster, moving in time with her breathing. Then they pulled away, turning, toward the bed. Winston and Maw. Winston and Maw. Over and under they swayed in through the window. Parting then touching. Parting then touching. Their dance was the same. Coming so close that one was the other. Creating a blanket that darkened the bed.

Lillie got off the bed, her shadow stretching long, crossing over Winston and Maw lost in the moon lines dancing on the far wall. Lillie edged past the shadows and walked out the door.

Winston? Winston, I know you're in there. She hit her fist against Jacob's bedroom door. I know why you got this door closed.

Oh God, Jake. She's coming in here. I told you we should've been quiet. The voice lay low in the water, close to the bottom, sinking deeper each time she spoke.

I saw you dancing, Winston. I saw you on the porch. Maw, I heard Paw come home last night. He left after the rooster.

No, Lillie. Go to sleep now, child.

Mother, what is it?

Open this door. You can't stay all night in this corn crib. They's rats in there, Winston. You come on out now.

Jake, where'd you put my clothes?

The voice dropped deeper, bent over, somewhere away. Away from where Lillie had been before Myrna went away. She should've taken her clothes. We laid the baby away in her christening gown. I should've put some clothes in the box, Winston.

Don't let your mother come in here. My God, Jake. Do something.

Just be still, Angie. Go back to bed, Mother. Dad's not in here.

I know you're in there, Winston. You and your trollops. All this time 'cause I didn't speak, you thought I didn't know. Unlock this damn door.

Mother, stop that cussing. And stop pounding on the door. You go back to bed. Now, Mother.

No. They's rats on the ceiling. And they's shadows dancing in there. I won't live in no tree.

What tree? What're you talking about.

78

Jake?

Just shut up. I'll take care of this.

Lillie slammed the door against the wall and stepped into Jacob's bedroom. Light down the hall dropped her shadow, like a hand stretched flat, across Jacob's chest.

I'll raise your boy, you whore. I'll call him mine 'cause I lost my own. Barren at fifteen ain't much to offer, but Winston's my husband. He ain't yourn.

The woman sat up in bed, straight, stiff, then rolled off the far side. She lay naked on the carpet. Lillie could hear her breathing.

Winston brought Jacob home to Lillie when he was three weeks old. He laid him in the cradle that had ten years earlier held the dying child. He's my son. We'll raise him in place of the other, Winston said. He dropped the baby's clothes on the kitchen table.

Lillie had said nothing. Of a generation raised not to question, she picked up the child. It turned its head to suckle her breast. She slipped her ring finger into its mouth and felt a tug in her loins as he pulled.

I'll call him Jacob. For Paw. She cuddled the child close against her body. She helped him form and never told Jacob about the moon shadows.

Jacob? Is that you?

Mother, what're you saying?

You can't bring your whore on to my Paw's place, Winston. Not even if Maw did give it to the both of us. He's been a good boy, Winston. I loved him hard. I kept him away from shadows all these years.

Mother. Mother. Mother. Jacob's voice was garbled under the dark.

Jacob, they's oranges in this room. I can smell them when the dark comes in.

Go back to your room, Mother.

Don't close me up in no room with no moon shadows, Jacob. They move in on you. Come right to your bed. You can't stay in here in the dark. Where's the light?

Damn, Mother. You're wearing me out. You've got to quit wandering around. Give me your hand. You want orange juice we'll get you orange juice. Come on. Let's go find your bear and we'll go back to bed.

# Carter's Woman

She leaves Carter standing on the platform, the little wooden casket tucked under his arm like rolled up newspaper, waiting by himself for a going-somewhere train. Going somewhere else. To lay their baby, her Henry T, in the hard, cold ground.

If she'd carried the coffin, she would have carried it before her bosom, cradled in her arms like a treasured silver tray crowded with fine blown crystal she'd seen once in a Birmingham store window. Brilliant glass that makes its own color when it can't hold the sun.

Unable to face the on-coming train, she leaves Carter. Her shoes drag over boards oiled smooth against the dirt. In the distance, smoke from the underground mine fire drops a haze over tree tops. She's going that way.

Walking between split fence rails, she imagines Carter on the train, sitting alone in the box car, probably on an overturned carton. The baby rests on Carter's knees as he rubs his hand over rough boards, trying to remember the gentleness of Henry T's face already leathering in the dark. Carter cries. He puckers his lips, then the cry moves across his face like hot summer wind. Agony overpowers him so completely he drops his forehead into calloused hands. When the train gets out of town, knowing him, he'll brace the coffin against his body so train-rocking won't nudge his son. Carter'll keep the baby safe. He promised her so.

Before Henry T's birthing here in this new place, she'd been lost. She sorted time between Ona, who at two years waddled underfoot waiting to be stepped on, and Carter Junior, CJ, a lanky nine-year-old, already angry at life trapped by coal dirt and clapboard shacks.

Hopelessness locked itself to her when Doc gave up on restoring Henry T less than a year after he was born. It bends her body and drags her soul out before her in a long, flat shadow. She now knows loss that had only hinted at existence before Jessup men came, before her Henry T died.

She left CJ this morning with word to watch Ona while she went with Carter, and, if necessary, to tuck Ona's dress tail under the bedpost to keep her inside.

"Go back with me," Carter'd said before leaving for the train. "We'll start over some place else."

Pride refused to let hate cast her out. "Ain't done nothing wrong. Henry T done no more an die, and he done that quiet. They's nothing to be afraid of. Here's your work. And it's good work and true. So I stay till you get the baby in the ground on your family's own plot. We'll weather this. Superstition won't run me off."

"It's hating us they ain't," Carter argued. "They's scared. And fear weighs heavier on the heart than any hate." But she wouldn't hear of leaving.

She believes Henry T would've probably made it, as least for a time more, if old Midwife Parsons hadn't left him unattended. She would've been willing to lie in her own blood to have him just a while longer. But Midwife, who Carter paid better than most coal camp fathers, grabbed Henry T's stiff legs and pulled him out, feet first.

She bellowed in pain and bled, split open like a butchered cow. Parsons laid him aside, unswaddled, blue and slick, and packed her tight to stave off the loss. "Reckon he's stillborn," Parsons said. When Carter finally caught her at the commissary, Parsons claimed her craft true and mumbled, "Shame the little one weren't born dead, seeing as how he is and all."

"Should've killed Parsons 'fore she got out of the house," she told him this morning. "Should've shot her or rung her neck like a worn-out fighting cock. Stopped her 'fore she spread her poison against Henry T."

"Leave it be," Carter told her. "Can't undo what's been done." He kissed the top of her head.

Late August sun burns her scalp. She lifts wet hair off her neck and drops it, splat, against her skin. Ahead, privet hedge, wilted from a week of days near a hundred and nights not much better, marks the road to the Lovett place. She starts up the rise.

Razor, Lovett's blue tick hound, meets her as she comes within sight of the house and trots up the road with her. She calls out, "Hallow the house. Can I draw me a drink a well water?"

Ruth Lovett, barely six, shrieks as she runs from the side yard. "She's in our yard." An arm appears and yanks Ruth through the door. Inside, a latch falls. A sawed-off 12-gauge shotgun slides out the window, pointed directly at where she stands.

"Get off my place. We don't got no water for you," Pa Lovett calls. "Don't need you poisoning my well or hexing my woman. Go back the way you come."

"I'm just asking for a sip of water, Pa Lovett. You know me. Carter's woman. It's a hot walk back to the house. My throat's awful dry."

"You ain't welcome here."

"Is she a witch, Ma? Is Razor hexed?" It's Ruth inside. "She petted him. I seen her do it."

The door cracks and a tomato, too ripe for slicing, hits her on the shoulder and drops into the dust. She picks it up, wipes the dirt away and bites. On the main road, she sucks juice and seed from the fruit.

CJ'll be hungry by now. Breakfast biscuits and cold sweet potatoes don't seem to hold him no more. She'll fry up some bacon and make thicknin' gravy to pay him for watching Ona.

When she left, he'd said, "Paw coming back?"

She said, "Not today."

"You coming back?"

"'Fore dark," she answered.

The first wave of men folk had come in good dark. Henry T, a few days old, was old enough for old Midwife Parsons to get her word out. Carter met them on the porch. "Stay inside," Carter had said. "It'll be men talk. You don't need to know it."

A month later when mineshaft number three shut down for a fire in the hole, men were back. She lay abed listening through the open window.

"Carter," Superintendent Oakes said, "we ain't knowed you and yourn long, but you seem to reason. What we've been hearing makes us wonder if you're what you set us up to believe."

"Don't know what you're saying, Super," Carter answered.

"Hard worker, we give you that," another said.

"As Superintendent, I give you the canary to tote in against fumes," said Oakes.

"I reckon so. Weren't no fumes when . . ." Carter answered.

Oakes interrupted. "It's this here baby she birthed. It's said he ain't got no strength in his legs, and he's got, well, to put it blunt, a place for . . . " Oakes stopped.

"Go on."

She could tell by his voice Carter was riled.

Nobody answered.

"Say what you come to say. Or get off my porch," Carter demanded. "Job or no."

A new voice, younger than the others, spoke up in a rush. "Midwife Parsons says his head's big as a watermelon, and he's got a tail place, raw and swoll up, covered up with hair for to hide it. Word has it he might be . . . " Like Oakes before him, the boy stopped.

"What?" Carter growled, his voice lower than she'd ever heard. "Be what? Answer me, Kid. 'Fore I come off this here porch."

"Old lady Parson said it," he stammered. "Not me."

"What'd she say?" Carter demanded. Carter's boots moved across the porch.

She visioned him near the edge.

"It's the devil's child. Ain't never seen nothing like it in all her midwifing." The ump had vanished, but he kept up his story. "Said she didn't die. Any other woman would've. And now with the mine afire, it seems to reckon . . . "

Carter stopped him. "You Oakes's boy, right? Doc don't think he's no devil child. Says he's got a 'condition.' His tailbone ain't right's all. Ain't closed up proper. He mote not walk. If anybody's a demon, it's Old lady Parsons. She nigh on to killed my wife. Look to that devil woman, if you want somebody to charge." He stalked into the house, slamming the door.

"Carter?"

He didn't answer.

She spits the tomato core into the ditch. Grit on the tomato twists her stomach; she bends over and vomits. Wip-

85

ing hands across her mouth, she hurries toward Simpson's Creek bridge, the last mark before home. The bridge, with its planks cool on her feet, lies just ahead.

Doc stayed Henry T's final day and night, not doing no doctoring. He set out front smoking with Carter, pitched ball with CJ, swung Ona when she whimpered. Said his hands was tied. Nothing he could do but wait it out. Had to go on living in Jessup. "All of Jessup's not superstitious. Some things you just don't change," Doc said.

Her grief didn't want him there, but Carter said seeing as how the camp felt like it felt, they needed a level head about.

After Henry T passed, Carter told her about finding hex signs scratched on the mailbox after Henry T's birthing. He told her about Old Tom hung in a tree, when before he'd told the kids some dog killed the cat, seeing as how he'd got so rickety.

"This ain't nothing more'n a witch hunt," she argued. "What can they do to us?"

"It's Henry T, not us. Doc says Oakes' boy aims to burn the baby and spread his ash so's his poison'll be gone. Doc's Doc. He's thinking he might talk down a mob. We need to get Henry T out 'fore they know to come back."

She refused to take it in. Throughout the night, she'd held her baby's swollen head to her bosom, though he'd not suckle. On toward morning, his head drooped and she knew he was dead. She felt him crumble like dried out plaster under her hands, and she folded up inside. For the first time, she saw his ashy skin and understood.

Carter had to take him away. And she would walk with him and Henry T to the train.

*"Not have my baby throwed on no bonfire 'fore little-minded people. While Carter's gone with the burying, I'll*

*make ready to let go this camp."* Her resolution quieted her for a time.

Carter and Doc had hammered out a little wooden box in the dark. With light of day, she bathed the baby, dressed him, and, denying the heat, wrapped him in a flannel blanket. While she dressed her baby, she recollected the birthing of CJ and Ona.

Holding her deformed son against her chest, her breasts throbbed with pent-up milk yet her loins hardened against birthing for such a wicked world. After a long rocking-time, she and Carter walked together, Carter toting Henry T in his wood box, to the train station. They left Doc, with her two children, behind.

Dirt burns through her shoes. It's like the ground itself is afire. She welcomes the bridge's coolness. The plank bridge sits a good twenty feet above the creek. Below, between cracks left to make for flexible crossing, water settles, forming a broad pool. She looks between the cracks, then sits on the edge, her feet high over the water. Dusty shoes dangle off her toes.

Distance tricks her eyes. Water appears to rise, right under her feet. She feels she can step out on the water and walk across blue-silver catfish gliding under her, the bank no more than a black line separating the real world from its reverse. Alone on the bridge, her head floats.

The voice of Henry T, now aged with wisdom, calls her mind. *"Step out on the water,"* she hears him say. *"Hover butterfly-like above this overturned world. Take freedom you haven't known since I first stirred in your belly. Drift with the water. Away from mine roofs that collapse. Away from woodsy ghost smoke that boils up from cracks and burns your* eyes. *Leave this smoke that stinks like Hell's sulfur, the stench of old men and their milky gas. Soar with me, Mama. Away from this poisonous place."*

An almost-smile of what her child could have been cuts across her face and forces out a whimper. With it comes the first release since her baby uttered his initial tinny cry. She drops her head and sobs.

After a weeping time, she rests. Below her, a gar slits the water. He gulps minnows before him as they dart past a bank outcropping of coal. Before the river's ridges reach the bank, their rippling circlets break.

From the direction of her house, there's coughing, a deep-seated hacking common nowadays to Jessup's black-lunged people. She looks toward her house, toward CJ and Ona, her hand shading her eyes against the Western sun. Just beyond the trees, a fat, dingy column of smoke rises. Wood smoke, not coal smoke.

Dropping her shoes, she runs barefoot, blind up the road.

A half-growed man stops in her path. "There she is, Pa. Let's get her."

She tries to dart pass. Oakes' son raises an arm to strike.

Behind them, CJ, bare feet dancing against leftover midday ground heat, tugs Ona, rumbling along in his self-made wagon.

"Ma?" he shouts. He stops the wagon. "Where you been? Somebody set the barn afire."

Ona begins to climb out of the wagon.

"Stay, you two," she shouts. "Where's Doc?"

"Gone to birth the Boss's new calf."

Eyes darting back and forth, Oakes' boy steps off the

road. Before he reaches the ditch, the ground beneath him crackles and pops as if it's alive.

CJ calls out in gulps. "Where you been, Ma?"

His hair, too golden to take in the sun, glistens with reflections. Remembering the Birmingham glass, she's blinded by CJ's fairness. Love for her son surges through her milk-laden breasts, and she realizes that what's lovely don't need no sun. It gives off its own light.

Lymon Oakes' spit, splattering dust on his already covered shoes, draws her back to the men. "Run on, woman. Don't you leave nothing behind but tracks in the dirt."

Mouth set, she stares into his eyes, their coldness enough to chill her insides. She glares till he gives way and drops his head.

With a creaking sound, behind Oakes, the ground opens. His boy's weight sends weeds, dirt, and rocks into the orange belly of the mine. Heat boils up and singes her face. Oakes' son grabs a pine sapling to stop his drop, his screams echo off creek banks behind her.

Oakes runs to draw him out. She gets there first. She strips off her blouse and loops it around his wrists, a handle for pulling. Bare-breasted, she tugs against the burden. Her milk-heavy breasts draw her forward. The boy inches into the hole. With no foot hold, he loads her down. She braces herself against red rip-rock cuts in her heels and heat scorches from burning underground coal.

Oakes steps tenderly over crumbling ground. He takes hold of the blouse and pulls his son out. The boy sits in the road, his soles blistered, tears striping smut on his face.

Oakes offers her blouse and mumbles, "I can't say nothing . . ."

"I know you, Lymon Oakes. You talk big in the dark." She slips her arms into the blouse and fastens the buttons as unconsciously as if she had just nursed Henry T.

Her back straight as steel, she yells to the woods, the creek, these men. "My name's 'Justine.' It ain't 'Woman.' And you, there in Mr. Boss Man's pocket, you tell your boy it ain't 'She.'"

Naming herself aloud warms her body. The roar of her own voice drowns the sound of water running behind her and releases the hardness inside her breasts. Henry T.'s milk dampens her blouse. With open hands, she smoothes the cloth as deliberately as when she irons wrinkles from work shirts.

Her head high, Justine steps out past the men and walks toward home. She takes her children's hands and leads them toward the horizon's wood smoke to box up their belongings.

## Loyalty

"I looked at his grave and, with tears in my eyes, I voiced these words: "You were worth it, old friend, and a thousand times over." - Wilson Rawls, *Where the Red Fern Grows*

# Chicken Bone

For Julian
POW, WWII

The dampness inside Noah's twelve-year-old Chevy truck intensified the reek of urine. Dog pee. Jena's rat terrier, Bella. No scrubbing, short of bleach, removed the stench. He had thought of trading the truck, but nobody wanted it. Town men teased and snickered. "Smell that truck before we see it coming," they said.

Noah rubbed his sleeve across the foggy windshield. Damn rain. You would think after all these years of fighting Alabama Februarys, he would get past this frustration that hit when he was caught with no cloth to dry off the mist. He swiped his shirtsleeve across the glass again.

In the cleared spot, a man appeared. Clad in a thin plaid shirt and army trousers, his shoulders were drawn up against the cold wet. Noah stomped the brake and yanked the steering wheel to the left. The truck bed slid toward the man. Noah fought the wheel. "Shit," he said under this breath.

The gangly man turned toward the headlights and tugged at an untrimmed mustache. Noah rolled down the passenger window. Rain blew in, further wetting Noah's sleeve. He leaned over to see if the man was who he thought he was.

"Clint? My God. Clint, is that you?" Thunder blocked out any answer the man might have given. "I could've killed you."

Clint walked away from the truck.

Noah threw the gear into neutral and set the brake. He jumped out into the downpour, grabbed the man's arm and twisted him around so he could see him face to face.

95

"Thought I was seeing a ghost in all this wet." When Clint didn't answer, Noah said, "Get in the cab. You're soaked."

Clint yanked his arm from Noah. Noah seized his half-brother by the back of his shirt collar and pushed him into the truck. Clint dropped a soggy Piggly-Wiggly paper sack of belongings on the floorboard. Noah shifted into first and edged back on to Highway 12.

"Man, I thought I'd never see you again." Noah shook his hair like a dog fresh out of a pond. "Leaving like that. Where you been all these years? Nobody's seen hide nor hair of you." Noah squinted and leaned forward. He knew this road, but he wiped the windshield again. His sleeve was now so wet it did little good.

Clint stared through the rain-streaked window at a stand of stick-like pines. He knew they wouldn't prosper. Too close together. Even as a kid, Noah always pushed things. Now the pines. One right up against the other.

At the dead-end sign, Noah turned onto the road. Gravel pinged against the underside of the truck. He killed the motor.

"I'm getting out," Clint said.

Noah strained to hear him over raspy wiper blades. "We're going home. Jena'll have us some supper. A hot bath. Good night's sleep." Noah slapped Clint's thigh and nodded. "Just like when we was kids."

"I ain't going." Clint reached for the door handle.

"'Course you going," Noah insisted. "It's your home, too, I reckon."

"Not no more." Clint's voice had a flatness in it Noah didn't remember.

"Don't be talking like that, Clint." Noah reached into his shirt pocket for a Chesterfield and match. "Things'll be better this time."

Clint grunted. "Why'd you stop the truck then if you're so sure I'm going?" he asked. He tapped his left leg up and down. After the constant battlefield noise in Korea, silence made Clint antsy.

Noah drummed his cigarette against the dash. "Thought you might be needing to make up your own mind, seeing as how I drug you into the truck and all." Noah lowered his window a crack and lit the cigarette. He blew smoke into the rain. "No matter me wanting, it's still your life you living."

Noah coughed deep inside his chest. Clint rapped his fingers across his thigh as if picking out a forgotten song on a guitar. He waited.

Noah leaned toward Clint. Smoke blew out Noah's nostrils. "'Member that night when you was fourteen? Fifteen? Snowing like hell. Jena and me, we met you running like a wild man down the middle of the road? Old man Smitty on your tail. Bet he'd skint you alive if you hadn't hopped into the bed of my old truck." Noah chuckled. "Moved his still, he did. 'Fraid you'd tell." Noah stopped talking and listened to rain plinking on the metal cab. "Didn't know you much, did he?"

Clint clutched his fingers into a fist and pounded his thigh. He laughed. "This shitty truck stinks."

"I reckon it does," Noah grinned and stomped the starter. Noah's wet shoe slid off the clutch. The truck rolled down the hill, and the motor kicked in. "Let's get in the dry."

The scent of hot lard and fried chicken met Noah as he crossed the threshold. Jena had her back turned. He knew, by the set of her shoulders, that she had seen Clint.

"He will not come in this house," she whispered.

"He's family."

97

"Just barely." Jena dumped washing powder into the sink. She grabbed the frying pan and attacked the grease where she had fried the chicken.

"No gravy tonight?" Noah asked.

At Jena's feet, Bella crunched her food. He looked at Jena's terrier hunched over her bowl. Massive ears, thin, rat-like face splotched in orange and white, rock-hard body and skinny tail. He wanted to grasp that tail and sling her out the window. "Damn dog. Got no business eating in the kitchen." Jena shrugged. "She's my baby."

Ask and Noah will admit he had babied Clint for years. Clint was the only brother he had, even if he was a half. Noah, five years older, cut Clint slack by doing his chores. Lied to their old man to keep him from throwing Clint out when he didn't come home nights. Slipping an extra dollar or two into Clint's pocket, knowing Clint would drink it up before the week was out.

Noah recalled a Clint who followed nobody's rules. He allowed no temperament to slow his actions. His life had been lived within a copse of prickly cedars, with Clint appearing and disappearing, leaving only a broken gap behind—a gap that closed before anyone could enter. Then Clint met North Korea.

And look what it had all come to. School dropout. Stint in Korea. Pistol whipping Buck Hobson nigh on to death. Then walking off without a word. Crazy restlessness, now so deep-rooted, he couldn't settle.

Jena leaned into the counter. She waited for Noah to give her justification for bringing his brother into her house.

Rather than give her time for a thought to come together, Noah reached around her waist and laid his head against her neck. "Come on, Hon. We can't leave him out in the cold. Think about what he could've been through."

She twisted, but he held her snug. "He's been Lord knows where. With Lord knows who." She whispered, as if she suspected Clint might be eavesdropping. "No word. No nothing. Since that fight over Buck Hobson's woman. What? Six years back?"

"I won't let no harm come to you." He kissed her behind the ear. "I'm right here, Baby."

Her body softened.

"What if Bella don't like him?' she asked as she pulled away.

"Nothing'll happen to Bella." He nibbled her ear. She faced Noah and wagged her forefinger near his rounded nose. "Absolutely no whiskey. I know he's a drunk and they're saying on the television that drunks can't help it, but I won't stand for no drinking in my house."

Noah nipped at her finger and grinned.

"One week, Noah. That's all. One week."

Noah, his hand against Clint's back, nudged him into the kitchen. A chipped enamel-topped table sat in the middle of the wall. Three mismatched chairs filled the open sides. Noah felt Clint's back stiffen when he saw that what had once been his place was now closed off, shoved against the wall.

Noah pointed to the chair across from where Jena would sit, where their Papa used to sit, leaving Noah his stepmother's place.

"Just like old times, right, Clint?" Noah said.

"Reckon so." Clint did not look up.

Jena plunked the bean bowl down on the metal tabletop. Then a plate of cornbread. Her knife struck the plate and crunched the crisp crust as it sliced into the pone. Smell of sweet corn drifted up from the bread's opening. She placed a platter of fried chicken legs in the table's center.

Noah slid the chicken platter toward Clint before reaching across the table for beans, bread, and onion slices. Noah spooned pinto beans in bite after bite then sopped up bean liquor with his bread. His mouth full, he pulled the last of the meat off his chicken leg with tobacco-stained teeth. Metal against crockery and Bella's crunching on dry dog food accentuated the silence. Noah and Clint leaned over their plates, chewing. Noah reached for another chicken leg.

"Where's your fork?" Jena spoke without opening her lips.

Noah drew back his hand. "Damn, Jena, I ain't no five-year-old." He picked up his fork and stabbed another leg so hard the fork rang against the platter.

"Stop it," Jena demanded. "You want to break my good dishes?"

Noah twisted in his chair. His elbow pushed the stripped chicken bone to the floor. He ignored it and dropped another leg on his plate, changed his mind, and put it back on the platter. He downed a glass of sweet tea and pushed his chair away from the table.

After eating, Noah pulled Clint down on the couch to watch Gunsmoke. "Ain't no better show on television," he said between cigarette puffs. "Been watching it since '55. Three years. It gets better ever week."

Clint rose to move to a chair, but Noah caught his arm and pulled him back down. "He ought to marry that Miss Kitty, don't you think," Noah said, not expecting a response. What he said was not to be questioned.

After the program, Noah gave up on trying to decide why the New York reporters had come to Matt Dillon's town looking for a story anyway, butting into somebody else's life like that. "Ain't no reason in anybody roaming over the country looking for trouble," he mumbled.

When Clint didn't answer, Noah said, "Might as well go on to bed." He stubbed his cigarette out in a thick glass ashtray, stood, and stretched. "What can you do with a man like Dillon?" Noah said. "Liquor, women, fights."

Clint ignored him. He removed his shoes, gathered a blanket from the back of the couch, and covered his legs. "Night," Noah said. Once Noah left the room, Clint pulled the blanket to the floor and lay down to sleep.

The first thing Noah saw when he entered his bedroom was a hump on the bed. Knowing what it had to be, he threw back the spread. "Good Lord." Bella lay on her belly, next to a mushy pile of undigested food. He slung the spread to the floor. He swatted the dog's rump, and she jumped off the bed with a yelp. Noah wadded the dirty blanket and tossed it on the floor. "Jena, get in here," he demanded.

Jena met Bella at the door and cradled the dog to her breast. "Poor baby. Have a widdle tummy ache?" She kissed Bella on the head. "Mommy get you some tum-tum medicine. Don't let that bad old man scare my baby," she grumbled on toward the kitchen.

Disgust settled over Noah. He mumbled as he crossed the room. "Baby brother struck dumb, won't talk. Why'd he come home if he didn't plan to be family? Jena loving on a ratty old dog. You'd think it was a kid instead of a dog. Years since she'd put her head to my breast."

Inside his bedroom closet, Noah reached behind his shirts for his camouflage coveralls. From an inside pocket, he pulled out a flask of vodka. He downed the alcohol easy, as if it were water. He crawled under the sheet and wiggled around to settle into a place for sleeping.

Down the hall, the TV squelched as electricity rushed into the room now that stations had shut down. Clint sat upright. He shuddered. It was two-way radios on the battlefields of Korea all over again. He blinked and blinked again to drive that memory away. He propped his back against the couch and stared at the screen, mesmerized at the test pattern of circles inside circles, each broken by four wide intersecting bands. The black lines made his eyes water. His hands shook.

A knothole in a board he had slept on in the prisoner of war camp in North Korea had met him each night, eye-to-eye. He would put his eye so close to the hole that when he rose he had a dent around his eyeball. He often wondered if he could carve out a hole big enough to see who slept under him. For three years, he would sleep no more than ten inches above another human being. The POW became nothing more than another face. They never spoke. He learned that to break a rule meant a bloodletting. He learned that rule early on—eight days after he was captured.

Four Korean soldiers had rushed into the barrack, jabbering words Clint barely grasped. "Soldier from Alabama talking," he thought they said. At first, he couldn't breathe. They meant him. He was from Alabama. They pulled a POW, a kid no more than twenty, out of the group. Clint hadn't heard anybody talking, but he kept his mouth shut. Clint wrapped his arms around himself and balled his fists to stop the trembling. The kid was bound with rope and dragged out of the wooden building. The four ordered the POWs outside of the building.

Outside they tied him to a stripped pole and riddled the boy with bullets. He never uttered a sound as his body bounced and jerked from the firing squad. They gouged him to prove he was dead, and then they laughed. His head hung low. He stood in a pool of blood, supported only by the ropes that help him to the pole. The soldiers forced the POWs back inside and locked the door. Clint lay stone still throughout the night.

The next morning as the POWs marched past the hanging boy, a thin mist blew from his nose as he breathed, indicating a whisper of life left there. A winter wind from Siberia had hopped mountain over mountain and scotched his blood flow. He would lose a lung, an arm from the elbow down, and both his balls, but he lived. The kid later said he lived so he could talk about it. After the war ended, Clint would testify to what he had seen. He finished his witness with: "No need to talk about this no more." And he had not.

After that shooting, Clint lived a life of "what ifs." What if he had had a knife? What if he had more to eat so he could have strength to run the cornfields after he wormed under the wire? And tonight? What if tomorrow his sister-in-law woke up half-human? What if his brother . . . ? But he had none of these answers. Staring into a black television screen could make a fellow go blind.

Just after dawn, Noah dragged himself into the kitchen. "Where's Clint?" he asked, scratching his bare chest.

"Where's Bella?"

"She's around somewhere. Probably under something." He poured a cup of coffee. "Still raining?"

He glanced out the kitchen window. The rain had slacked a bit, but it rained nonetheless. He saw Clint squatted next to the chicken coop. A shovel leaned against the pine trunk. "What's he doing out there?"

Jena drew closer to the window to look.

At the far edge of the backyard, Clint crouched on his knees, bent over a pile of dirt. His plaid shirt stuck to his skin. Next to his knee lay a lumpy blue shirt. He lifted it with both hands, as if cradling a baby, and placed it in a hole. He guided muddy dirt over the hole with his hands and tamped it, first with his hands then with his fists.

Jena let the kitchen door slam and ran screaming across the yard. "Murderer!" She threw herself on Clint's back. Her weight flattened Clint face-first into the mud. Noah grabbed Jena at her waist and heaved to get her off his little brother. She flailed her arms and legs, kicking Clint's hips, his back, and Noah's shins with her hard-soled oxfords.

She shouted at Clint, "You SOB! One turn and she wiggled out of Noah's hands.

"Shut up," Noah shouted. "That's enough." He groped again, grabbing whatever he could grasp.

Jena shrieked in pain and rolled off Clint. She turned on Noah and beat his chest with her fists. "What do you mean, grabbing my tit like that?"

"God, Jena," Noah said. "You gone crazy?"

"He's done killed Bella." She slapped Noah hard across the face. "I told you not to let him stay."

Behind her, Clint smoothed the center of the mound and rose from the mud.

Noah gripped her wrists. "Stop it, Jena."

She fell against him, breathing hard.

"He killed Bella," she whimpered.

"Big Brother, you ought not feed a dog chicken bones," Clint said, his back to his family. "They sliver. Little dog died from inside."

Noah felt his pants for a cigarette. There were none there. "I didn't feed . . ."

Jena spit her words toward Clint. "I knowed all along you was a no-count." She squatted down and threw a metallic

104

object off the mound and evened the soil. "Noah should've left you on the side of the road to die."

"Now, Jena." Noah stroked her shoulder. She pulled away.

Clint picked up his paper sack and took the muddy shovel. Jena cowered over the little grave and watched him wide-eyed. Clint beat the shovel against clay stuck to the sole of his shoe. He stuffed his Piggly-Wiggly paper sack, now empty, into his pants pocket. He stepped over Bella's grave and cut between Noah and Jena.

Rain has a unique trick of falling in one place. The rain and the sun appear to battle for the right to claim some invisible barrier. It allows folks to walk into the rain and back out again. Often for no particular reason, other than the thrill of controlling what people do.

Noah moved out of the rain and away from Jena. He picked up the medal piece, now washed clean. He held a bronze cross, no more than two-inches high with an eagle on the center and a scroll beneath. The scroll read "FOR VAL-OR." Noah flipped it and read Pvt. Clint Townsend. "Oh, baby brother." Noah's words struggled for air. Something viscous lodged in his throat and held his words at bay. "Why didn't you say so?" He put his brother's Distinguished Service Cross in his pocket. The patch of rain moved over and fell again on Noah.

In the distance, Clint climbed the road toward the highway. Before he reached the crest of the hill, he brought out a whiskey bottle, turned it up, and drank it dry. He threw the empty bottle toward a pine's black trunk. It hit its target and shattered into a brown explosion.

From beside Bella's grave, Noah called out, "We need to talk!" Clint walked on. Noah twisted around and glared at Jena. "I need me some hard liquor," he said.

"Don't you dare." Jena said it almost like a gasp. She seized Noah's arm.

Noah wrenched her hand away. He stepped out of the rain, slamming the kitchen door as he went inside.

Dazed, Jena moved one foot. It fell on Bella's grave. Her shoe sank into mud. A rowdy hen squawked at her. Jena gagged from the stench of wet chicken shit across the wire fence. She untied her oxford and drew out her foot. One foot bare, she limped toward the kitchen.

By dusk, the rain had stopped. Noah heard a series of abrupt yips and a soprano howl from the back woods. A wolf pup stalking his chickens, he thought. "Going out to check on the chickens," he called to Jena. She didn't reply.

He hid his vodka bottle in the bib of his overalls. He walked easy. His bones ached from the tension of the past twenty-four hours. Outside, he swallowed a long draft of liquor and watched the sun shoot pink and purple clouds across the horizon. The coming dark didn't hold him back. He stumbled on. He needed to get as far away as he could so he could be alone with himself.

Near the chicken coop, he stopped as he approached the fence. Something shadowy sat atop Bella's grave. At first glance, Noah thought it was Bella herself, back from the dead. He paused next to the mound and rubbed his eyes. It wasn't Bella. It was a shoe. Jena's shoe, filled with rainwater. He bent to lift the shoe but ordered himself not to. "Leave it be," he said to nobody. "It won't matter none one way or the other."

# A Widow's Mite

Birds pick their mates mid-winter. Birds, yes, but not Leah. She chose Beau in early spring. Beau Townsend from Natchez down river was striking landed gentry, a man who could offer just what she, at eighteen, wanted.

Beau knew she loved her pets: puppies, kittens, rabbits, ducks. She had grown up cuddling them, burying her face in their tender fur and down, going to bed nights bathed in their woodsy smell. Before the wedding, he had promised her life in the country.

After the wedding, he moved Leah ten miles out from Copeland's Crossing, to the middle of nowhere. She told him, half joking, to live on the worn-out Alabama truck farm he'd inherited, one he preferred over her choice in town. This was his house, he told her, a house handed down, a legacy worth honoring.

After the wedding, Beau set out his collections. First, colorful butterflies stuck with bigheaded pins to paper under glass. Butterflies not unlike those Leah had coaxed to feed off her finger as a child. He centered his collection on Leah's grandmother's trunk in front of their sofa, then he stacked big trophy guns in a glass-fronted cabinet his father made when Beau was a boy. The rest he hung from angled deer hooves across the front wall—his bragging rights for anyone who entered his house.

Leah walks through the house, squeezing in her shoulders so as not to bump a weapon and send it shooting to the floor. A foolish thought, for she knows Beau never leaves loaded guns unattended. She looks first at his picture in the family room, then across and above the mantle to their wedding portrait. In it, he is standing close behind her, and she is seated with his hand resting on her shoulder. Inside, she's surrounded by trophies. Outside, brambles and weeds shelter snakes and lizards that scurry like spring lightning across the porch.

Beau hunts, evenings after work, weekends at the hunt club with "The Boys." Leah becomes a hunter's widow, truly as if her husband had been laid in the ground. When he is home, she's surrounded with reminders.

In an attempt to redeem the killing seasons and the gaps they leave, she bears a boy child. When Aaron is born, Leah locks off the gunroom and stuffs the key in a high bureau drawer.

Beau calls her silly. "A boy needs a gun," he says. "It makes him a man." He unbolts the gun cabinets. Alone with no one to back her, unlocking the cabinet pins Leah to the wall.

In Aaron's tenth year, Beau teaches him to shoot, straight and true.

It's February and an early evening storm is rising, one that makes Leah want to crawl in the storm cellar and lock the door behind her. Standing at the top of wooden porch steps, she watches Aaron and Beau, coming home from another hunt. Their orange caps balance for a moment across the back field, duplicate suns lighting the early dusk of a mid-wintry sky. Together, father and son advance through rows of brown stalks, as if returning from some ritual sacrifice, stepping among remnants of corn Beau tried to grow, seed for luring deer and quail.

The two, in some strange reversal, remind her of Abraham's Sarah, and she wonders if Sarah would have led that child up the mountain. Has she, equally as guilty as the ancient Jewess, betrayed her son by knowingly allowing him to follow his father? Would her sacrifice, like the widow's at the Jerusalem Temple, no matter how small, not be defaced by grander expectations?

Clouds, grey-bottomed and heavy, gather low behind the returning hunters as the late afternoon storm builds beyond the hill. Leah listens for the sizzle that signals the onslaught of lightning. Inner tension radiates through her body and readies her to reach out, grab her child, and run. She reprimands herself. Ridiculous, for she knows the most dangerous strikes usually come unpredictably. She has seen them before, their notice never creeping in but arriving with prominent pronouncements of horrific sound and light.

From her place on the porch, she sees the hunt bag, more pillow than sack, its soft leather puffed out by down and the weight of the kill. February weekends and Townsend land promises a hunt, then fried quail and grits, with Leah's bird cleaning stuffed somewhere in the middle.

She tells herself she is comfortable dressing tiny brown quail, a small sacrifice to offer her husband. But the attachment she made to one mother hen who marshals her covey out of the field and across the road to hide in blackberry tangles at back of the barn interrupts her concentration each time she lifts a tender bird out of the bag.

During each cleaning, as she rubs a finger down the feathers of the game Beau and Aaron bring in, the covey marches back across her mind. She thinks them beautiful, the hen and her chicks, all in a line, their feathers slick and as brown as Beau's over-creamed coffee. The quail's softness gentle on her skin, she and the hen and the need to guard her chicks, intertwine so intricately she cannot distinguish between the down on her arms and the feathers in her hand. With each sensation, she trembles.

Dropped from the bag, quail become just another meat, she reminds herself, and, though she tries and though Beau says, "Just skin 'em, Love," she wants to pluck them like chickens. To be able to pluck their feathers would make them fair game for food, it seems. Determined, she pinches and pulls, but finds the feathers so tiny, so baby-hair soft, they cannot be grasped. What she manages to pull off floats, as if caught in a breeze hosting far-lightning. They blow into the yard, rather than drop solidly into piles at her feet on day-old newspaper as chicken feathers do.

Now when she cleans, she still tries plucking from time to time, to prove that the quail are born to be plucked, to tell herself they were made for food, that they are merely wild creatures set down to walk lightly.

Jerk off their heads. Skin them and gut them. Take away their feathers. Force them into new-creature rank. Silent as she cleans, she orders herself to know these things. Work them like fowl, and quail will lie more like coop chicken, only smaller this time and sweeter on the plate.

Leah lifts her hand toward the field to call out "Hallo," but she is cut short by thunder clamoring, reverberating like clanging cymbals beyond the hill. Thunder in February means frost in May and a cold spring. Her grandmother told her this, and she does not question what her grandmother taught. There are guarantees in what is handed down.

Her voice is silenced by the on-coming storm, and she drops her hand as if exhausted. It falls limp against her thigh. She wonders at this lifelessness, the heaviness she is experiencing, this being smothered by the very air itself, and realizes it is Aaron. He is not here beside her to sustain her against the weariness. He's there, crossing the field with his father.

Somewhere in the back of her mind, Leah had hoped Aaron would be cut from a different cloth, that he would grow to speak for what she cannot.

She told him, "Crow's one thing. She'll mate with anything that comes along. Then she pushes the eggs out of the first nest she finds, claiming whatever she wants to be her own. Not so with quail. Their lives are so short. Six, seven months at the most." She pauses. "Not so with dove either. They mate for life."

"I know that. I'm not a baby."

"No, you're not." She reaches to push back his hair.

Aaron ducks. Turning away, he rushes his words. "You're asking me to chose, Mama, and that's not fair." He speaks with authority, not reprimand.

"No, it's not fair. But somehow we owe it to nature to protect her best," she answers. "That's all," she says, her voice made small by the knowledge of what she lays on her child. Then, lapsing into her grandmother's lessons, she tells him, "I don't want you to live out your life being one mite sorry about nothing, son. That widow," she reminds him, "gave all she had at the temple. She was laughed at for not giving more. I don't want to give you up. Not you or the birds."

But Beau trains him well, garnering deep within the boy a strong taste for the hunt. First turkey, then crow, now quail. Soon they will move to larger game. Deer perhaps, then black Delta hog that fear no hunters, that attack with tusks that slice and hooves that tear.

When Leah tried talking before, Beau passed her words off as if they were no more than rain showers, inconveniences like water staved off by cap flaps and thick boots.

In memory, she shouts at Beau, steeling his armor, her words wounding her pride, circling in on herself, forging a new person—someone she cannot recognize. Beau's ignoring her rants proves worse punishment than any uplifted hand.

Raising a boy to be more dove than crow is harder than hand-picking quail feathers. There is always a season, a season to kill. This day she knows, as she watches them approach the farm house, she has lost her son as surely as if Beau had marched him up the mountain and laid him, bound, on some primitive altar.

When this quail season first opened, Beau brought home a golden canary in a domed metal cage topped with a stiff red paper bow he had tied himself.

"Here's you an early Christmas present, Little One. You have your own bird." He smiled at her and kissed her gently on the forehead. "Now we're all set."

Leah named her bird Prissy and longed to set her free. She wanted Prissy to serve as some sort of appeasement for all the birds Beau had shot, all those he had yet to kill. But knowing the bird would stand no chance in the wild, she set her by the kitchen window, away from the door's draft.

Now on winter days warm with a promise of spring, she sets cage and bird on the flat, wooden porch rail so Prissy, like herself, can anticipate a new season.

Today, the false spring of an Alabama February calls Leah, summoning her to come, turn her face to the sun, the same way it calls snakes to leave their dens in search of first season heat. Clouds have moved in from the southeast, dark, as if they scraped the ground and came up covered with dirt—their heaviness trapping what should be next August's heat. They hover close, squeezing out oxygen between earth and sky. Ozone preceding the storm restructures the air, making it harder for Leah to breathe.

Slumped against the porch column, Prissy singing behind her, Leah watches her husband and son as they rejoice in their game, high-stepping homeward, their guns pointed behind them like two heavy, angled lightning rods daring nature to strike. She calls out to warn of the storm moving in low at their back, but before her voice reaches them, lightning sucks energy up from the soil and sends out a hissing haze shooting before itself. Electricity lifts the hair off Leah's arms, and thunder shakes the kitchen window panes.

At the field's edge, a sphere of crystal blue flame rests for a moment atop a black pine, and the thin tree fires as quickly as a match laid flat against a stove's hot eye. Lighting shatters the trunk, splitting it asunder.

Leah shouts, "Drop the damn gun, Beau!" Beau and Aaron fall in the dirt, Aaron's gun thrown before him.

Lightning splinters the air and thunder resounds, light and sound indistinguishable, echoing and blinding like a gunshot trapped in a closed room. The storm is upon them. The smell of burnt oxygen and boiled pinesap fills the air as dingy smoke rises from the burning tree.

Leah can't breathe. Before her, Beau and Aaron rise, their heads bent forward, not unlike roosters climbing a henhouse pole to dodge the rain.

On the porch rail, Prissy flaps her wings in irregular rhythm against the metal cage. The sound of the struggle sends a shudder charging through Leah, and she turns away from the field. There on the porch rail, solid as a piece of rusted steel, lies a chicken snake, the one she's seen at the barn, the one she told Beau about last fall, its body now winter lean. Drawn out by February warmth, the snake is still slow from January cold, but limber enough to coil. Ready to strike, his eyes stare, fixed on Prissy's fight with her cage.

113

Leah needs to run for a hoe, but she cannot leave the porch. The snake will sliver through the wires and swallow Prissy before she can get back. If she moves to grab the cage, he'll strike her. She knows the results of chicken snake bites, deep slices that demand hospital stitches. Her feet are rooted to the plank floor, her throat dry as last year's cotton, her voice vanishes.

Ignoring the on-coming storm, Aaron yells from his spot in the field, "Hey, Momma, look. We got a full bag today." He holds out the bag then slings it back, his personal honor cape, over his shoulder.

The snake edges his head closer to Prissy's cage and sways as if caught in a summer breeze.

With no time to kill, Leah cries out, her voice raspy, "Aaron, get the hoe. It's the chicken snake. After Prissy. Beau? Oh, Beau," she pleads. "Bring your gun." Her voice drops into a whisper, fear bending her double against the porch column.

Aaron picks up his gun and drops the game bag from his shoulder. It hits the ground, heavy and silent. Its fill of quail mounds it in place, so stable it sits upright on its own.

For days afterward, each time Leah steps out of the kitchen, she will imagine the dark heap in the corn field, a smoldering pine trunk glowing behind it.

Aaron runs toward the house, aiming his gun as he comes.

His father calls him back. "Don't you shoot into that house, boy. Your mother's there."

"It's Momma's bird, Daddy. It's Momma's bird," he calls and pauses in the run just long enough to pull the trigger.

Leah sees Aaron mark the house, but she's frozen. He shoots. Window panes above the porch rail crackle, split, and fall out of their frames, tinkling with summer wind chime music.

With the shower of glass, the snake follows itself off the rail, lands with a plop, and disappears under the porch. Inside the cage, Prissy drops from her swing into birdseed spilled in her terror, a tiny red streak on her breast. Another bird dead on yesterday's newspaper.

Leah drags herself to the porch rail, centered in an unending roll of thunder. She doesn't notice blood dripping down her leg from Aaron's birdshot. Instead, she wipes her cheek with the back of her hand and rubs the dampness from her face on her pants. Using her fingers, she pulls at her cheek as if smoothing her rouge and a pellet drops to the floor. Later when her face heals, people who don't know will pass the pocks off as some surface skin problem. Something at some time or other she had to learn to live with, they will say.

Leah loops a finger, gummy with blood, through the top ring and brings the cage level with her face. "Come on," she whispers to her bird. "We belong inside."

Beau shouts from the field, "Leah? Leah, you okay, Hon?"

She doesn't answer but walks into the kitchen. Framed by shards of broken glass, she looks back to the field. Conscious now of the burning pellet wounds from Aaron's shot, she drops Prissy's cage to her belly and lets it dangle before her. Across the field, Aaron goes back for the quail bag, raises, and swings it with a conqueror's air to his shoulder, then he runs toward the barn to beat out the rain. Beau drops his gun and tears through the field toward the house calling Leah's name.

Leah hugs the cage to her breast and waits, the wire painfully cool through her shirt.

Her husband reaches the porch as rain begins to pelt the roof. She hears him pause and inhale as if deep breathing will bear him more easily across the threshold. He steps into the kitchen and drops his orange cap on the floor, fright and remorse slashed across his face.

She cocks her head and looks at him, awed by how this day has accentuated, rather than marred, his rugged features. Leah lifts her hand to strike, but balls her fist and walks out the door into the rain.

# Waiting for the Pink

Horace Noland was rubbing coal oil into his elbow to fight off the lumbago when he heard the first shot. Just a little pop, not worthy of rising and moving to the window. Too stove up to try. Old scrap of meat throwed over some bones. That's what Willie Mae Blesser allowed ever time she put her thick wide arms round his middle.

The second shot pop-pop-popped like a repeating cap gun. Lawley, guess he best check out the commotion. Black man peeping out a black window into black night wouldn't be seen. Using his hand to boost his weight off the mattress, he stirred the air round him. When he moved, Horace laughed a high-pitched he-he-he and spoke out loud. "Well, Greenback, so old I don't even know the sound of my own fart. Willie Mae Blesser would of throwed a blue fit. 'Ain't nothing worse than a man who can't keep his own gas, Horace Noland,' she'd've said. Sure enough."

From the door sill, a slick green lizard watched as he edged himself off the naked mattress. So bent by age, he slid along with his head down, angled level with the ground. He seemed older than God himself. "Best I bent like a wind-broke tree," he said. "Folk looking straight on at me'd be scared shitless," he said, thinking 'bout the misplaced dimple deep in his upper lip. "Looks for all truth like I got me a third nose hole to my face," He chuckled again. "Ain't that the truth?" he said to the lizard. The lizard blinked and looked back.

"Gotta take a leak, Greenback. Get out my way 'fore I mash you flat," Horace said. As he rose from the bed, a trickle ran down his thigh and pooled dingy pink pee in his shoe. "Reckon I old. Can't even make it to the edge of the porch,

117

you lizard." He signed. "Where's that Willie Mae Blesser when I need her?" He dropped back onto the mattress and laid his angles across the bed. His feet, too heavy to lift off the floor, swung like matched pendulums, then stopped. His head pointing to the foot of the bed, his eyes facing the door, he pulled a wool crazy quilt over his arms and slept.

Before midnight, early March rain hit the roof all at once and a night full of acorns bounced like dancers across the tin. Later, tiny men in black and white stripes crawled up on his back, and, starting at his backbone, moved round to his hips, using steel hammers, and pounded sharp even nails into the flesh of his waist. In his sleep, he twisted and shivered trying to shake them off, but they stayed till they finished, then vanished.

He woke at daybreak, Greenback on the bed next to him, turned brown against a rusty quilt square. The door stood open, either because Horace had forgotten to close it before dark or because the wind came in during the night. Horace didn't remember.

Rolling over to gain leverage for sitting up, Horace groaned. "Done a fine job this time, you slimy old lizard, them chain gang mens. They fill me so full of aches my body done stuck in one place. Hum. Hum. Hum."

Greenback didn't move till Horace slapped the bed before him and said, "Scat."

Horace slid over to a sawed off barrel turned upside down to hold the electric eye for cooking. He scraped yesterday's oatmeal out of the black-bottomed pot and dumped it on his green plastic plate, then ate, using a knife to cut the oatmeal into chunks, spearing each bite into his mouth with the blade's tip. When he finished, he dropped a glob of cold oatmeal on the floor before the lizard.

Greenback scurried up the wall.

"Don't blame you, old lizard. Looks more like snot than food, I reckon."

A little before noon a white girl appeared in the door, as quiet as if Horace'd conjured her up himself. He'd been waiting for Willie Mae Blesser to come in from the kitchen with greens and corn pone all hot for the eating, so he jerked when she tapped a puny, white knock on the door frame.

Dressed in pale pink with glittery yellow hair, he thought she must be an angel, so he didn't speak, thinking his quiet'd make her stay, after a bit, she cocked her head, and Horace craned his neck to see if her wings showed. But nothing behind her shifted except a shadow throwed cross the porch by Willie Mae Blesser's dogwood.

When she said "You Mr. Noland?" with a question at the end, he knowed she weren't no angel. No self-respecting angel'd come to earth not knowing what she's about.

"If she ain't no angel, Greenback, she's apt to be a ghost. Lawley. Lawley." He slid across his naked mattress toward the wall, not thinking about lifting his feet.

"No sir," she smiled. "I'm not a ghost, and I'm certainly not an angel. I'm with DHR." She stepped across the sill. "Can I come in?"

"Looks like you are in," he said. Greenback skittered down the wall and hid behind the barrel half.

Seeing the lizard, the girl drew back.

"Ain't nothing but a lizard's all," Horace said. "Come in and set. Willie Mae Blesser ain't in here yet, but she's coming."

"I need to ask you some questions, Mr. Noland. It's reported that you might could use some services." Inside, she glanced at his face, and her face all at once like everybody

119

else's. Not looking at him, she slipped a black book and pen out of her pink bag.

"Don't reckon I'll be needing no services. Lawley. Now there's a service, so's I's told. Had my fill of services."

Still standing, the girl kept her eyes on her paper. "What's your full name, Mr. Noland?"

"Carver Horace Noland. Most folk round bouts calls me Horace."

"Horse? That's a strange name. Why would your mother name you Horse?" Glancing up, she smiled and shifted her weight to one foot.

Seems a might green to be working in this part of the county, Horace thought. Else she's poking fun. "Don't reckon she did," he said, not sure he liked this girl. "Wouldn't be no stranger than being named letters like you." He scooted himself up to the rim of the mattress so's he could put her out the door, if he saw fit.

"DHR's not my name." She laughed a real laugh this time. "I work for the Department of Human Resources. We can assist you with whatever you need to keep you safe and healthy." For the first time, she raised her eyes. *Bluer than my Lawley's baby blanket*, Horace thought. Looking at him this time, she didn't flinch. "My name's Barbara, and most people call me Barb." She offered him her hand.

Putting her pen in the pink bag, she stepped closer, her hand still out, a jingly silver bracelet rattling her wrist.

He looked past her out the door at Willie Mae Blesser's dogwood. Horace'd knowed eyes like that before, but they hid in dark cracks in his mind, and thinking now don't always let him dig deep into what's real and see what's not, not like he once done.

"Think you'd be blown away in last night's storm?" she asked.

He heard a broad smile in her words now. Without looking, Horace took her hand. It was warm and floppy, like shaking a wet washrag.

When Horace didn't answer, she continued. "I'm always skittish in storms myself."

"I ain't scared." He took his hand back, but he kept his face turned to the wall. "Some white women's scared to come in here. Scared I be jumping they bones." Horace cut his eyes toward her without looking at her straight on. "That Baptist do-gooder come in here and tacked a white Jesus up on my wall, now she be scared. Jumped like a kitten ever time I moved. You ain't scared?"

Barb walked over to the picture of Jesus, his hands open so everybody could notice his nail marks. "No sir. I'm more scared of that lizard crawling up my leg than I am of you." She laughed a chopped up laugh that had trouble coming out, then turned her back to the picture and faced Horace. Pointing to the lizard, she asked, "What's Miss Willie Mae Blesser think about him staying in here?"

Horace Noland figure'd he'd said enough. When he didn't answer any more of her questions, she left, saying she'd be back.

Judging by the wall calendar, she come by on the second box of ever week, first just talking, bringing him grocery, a jacket for next year's winter, then talking bout moving into town to a senior home. "Old folks home ain't for me," he insisted, and she'd drop it for a spell. Then she come by a cool weather morning catching him rubbing his kerosene, sitting next to his gas heater, and she'd start in again.

It took three calendar boxes for Greenback to cotton up to her. On a day so full of coming summer sun it burned your eyes, Horace spied the lizard moving cross the floor,

121

Barb not noticing, but talking like a greased wagon running in sand. When Greenback come nigh on to her slick black shoe, Horace spoke, quiet as the lizard, "Now, don't you shy none, but old lizard Greenback's nosing your toe. Just you be still while he sizes you up."

Without moving her head, Barb spotted the lizard with sidewise eyes. Only her eyes, round as the moon, moved. Horace told she could go ahead and breathe now. "He ain't aiming to hurt you. Lizard, he ain't got no teeth. He just like me. All gum." Horace laughed his he-he-he.

Barb let out her breath, reached down and ran her finger across Greenback.

"You finally come to a like-minded house, girl," Horace said with a grin.

Before month's end, she come to him in white. He saw her standing in the swinging door, its glass window cutting down one side, then lost her against the hospital wall. He didn't place her again till she spoke, her voice quiet and gentle, not a single thorn on the vine.

She told him his neighbor had no choice but to call the police when he saw Mr. Noland walking, gun loaded and ready, round and round his house. "Why do that, Mr. Noland? Don't you realize that going around with a loaded gun can get you in jail? Didn't I hear you were at Atmore for a time? Why on earth?" She'd reached the bed by the time she stopped asking questions and put her hand—damp, sticky, and soft—against his forehead. "The nurse says you have a serious kidney infection. Passing blood, even. You didn't tell me you needed a doctor. Are you better?"

He watched red and yellow cartoon frogs dancing in and out among trees and green bushes on the television set hanging from the wall.

Barb turned off the television. "Talk to me, Mr. Noland. You want to get back home. Greenback needs you."

"The county they come and say to me cut down that tree." He stopped.

"Go on," she encouraged.

"It's in the way of a wider road, they say." Without thinking what he was doing, he looked directly into her steel blue eyes. "Us chain gangers, we built them roads. I know what they takes, and they don't have to take no dogwood tree to make a road." He turned to the wall, talking now more to him own self than to her.

"Willie Mae Blesser, she planted that tree out by the road when we's just married. A sign for all to see she prided our home place. Brought it from the old Mrs.' own yard. 'The Mrs. give them to me, fair and square,' she said, 'for scrubbing her back steps clean. It's two. One white and one pink, and I aim to plant it both in the same hole.' And it growed strange, up together then split right down the middle. Like it was two trees with one root. And when it bloomed, one side showed white, white as snow in April. The other side waited for the white to die off and popped out pink, like it'd been stained by the blood from the death of the white. But my Willie Mae, she loved that tree. Waited in season for the blooming. She birthed our Lawley boy the one year the whites stayed on for seeing the pink." Horace rested, gathering energy for carrying on.

"And then some white strangers come on my land and say 'This ain't your land so near the road. This here land's the county's.' Say, 'Cut down this tree, or we'll do it ourself.'"

Her hand rubbed like cream cross his where it lay flat on the bed.

"Mr. Noland. Mr. Noland," she sounded tired.

123

"Nobody ain't taking down my Willie Mae's tree. Weren't I sick and abed, I'd be marching my yard still, guarding her tree." He jerked his hand back and wiped his eyes so she couldn't shame him by looking at his sorrow.

"I don't know what to do, Mr. Noland. You concentrate on getting well, and we'll see to the tree then."

"You go and set on my porch and see to it that tree ain't cut." He locked her eye and grabbed her hand, gripping it, pulling it to his chest. "You DHR. You come saying you here to help. You go now and do that one thing for my Willie Mae."

"I can't do that. That's breaking the law." She tried pulling her hand away, but he held strong. After a moment, she said, "If they cut your tree, I'll plant you another one. One just like it."

"Ain't nother one like it nowhere." He let go of her hand and turned his face away.

April nigh out of boxes when the blue policeman come in Horace's house without so much as a tap on the door. He took the gun and said, "Time to go, old man."

"Time? I done my time." Horace set on the edge of his naked mattress, staring at the floor. "Done my service. Service in World War 2. Service in Atmore and up and down them asphalt bubble roads. Pulling a chain waist to waist. I done it. Lawley. Lawley." Facing the plank floor, Horace shock his head.

"Yeah. You served well. Now come ahead peaceful." The police took Horace's elbow.

Horace pulled it away and cradled his left arm in his right, as if he held a newborn babe, kneading out the lumbago as best he could without a spot of kerosene.

"Service for twelve. Lawley still a lapbaby, he was. Service for twelve with a silver pie server. Willie Mae Blesser,

124

she brung it home. For polishing for old Mrs.'s Christmas party. Cause Lawley sick as a horse and needing his mama near by." Tears, spread out and wide, wet Horace's face, but the blue police had hold of his elbow so he couldn't wipe away the shame.

"What service for twelve, Mr. Noland?" Barb came in from behind the policeman. She kneeled down in front of Horace and smoothed the collar of his shirt, then rested her hand on his shoulder. "What're you doing here?" she asked back at the policeman. Without waiting for an answer, she spoke to Horace, "What're you talking about, Mr. Noland?"

"The Mrs., she say my Willie Mae kept her silver pie server."

"You DHR?" the policeman asked.

"No. Not anymore." She stopped and looked up at the policeman.

"Oh?" the blue police said, hoisting his eyebrow.

"They fired me, if you must know. I just come by." She turned back to Horace. "You want a pie server? I've got one I had since I was little. I'll give it to you," Barb said.

"Fired you, huh? What'd you do, slug this old stubborn coot?"

"Claimed she stole it for me to sell. Medicine for Lawley. That's all we wanted. But she never done it. I never sold none of it. Never seen it." Horace continued, shaking his head with every word.

"What?" Barb spun round to the policeman. Seeing his tobacco grin, she spoke through stretched lips. "No. I wasn't objective enough, it seems." She turned her back on him, squatting still, keeping her face leveled with Horace's.

"Got the medicine by loading the Mr.'s hay. But it never done no good. The Mr. he knowed where the money come from. Promised he'd do whatever it takes to make it right. But he never spoke for me at the courthouse. He set dumb and let me go off to Atmore and not stand by my Willie Mae at our Lawley's service. And he wouldn't speak for me again come time to leave Atmore for my Willie Mae with her dying of a busted heart. Busted wide open, they say, from grieving so." Horace stared eye to eye at Barb, thinking the Lord'll strike me dead looking straight on at a white woman and not caring.

"Come on now, Mr. Noland," the policeman said, twisting his arm to see his watch. "It's time for you to move on cross town. They've got you a fine room with a window and good food. You'll be right at home in no time."

"Ain't going." Horace kneaded at the pain his arm. "Damn elbow. Got chains on my bones."

"What'd he do this time?" Barb asked. "Why're you here?"

"Chained to this house I am. Chained."

"Shooting at the road crew this morning," he answered. "So they's a warrant. Most got that young kid what holds out the stop sign. Kid with green hair."

"Me and my lizard. Waiting for the pink."

"What the hell's he talking about now?" the officer blurted out, then stopped. "Sorry, Miss." Moving toward the door, he said, "Guess I need some air."

Barb lifted her bones off the floor, and her and the police walked out on the porch. Horace slid up behind them, counting on Barb to run the blue man off his land.

"It's his tree. The tree by the road," she said. "He's waiting for the pink side to bloom. His wife Willie Mae was buried the second week in April, when pink dogwood flowers bloom. Seems they're late this year."

The blue man nodded.

"White's almost gone now. Leave him here another week." She spoke in an almost whisper. "Once the pink blooms, I'll take him over. I'll do whatever it takes to make things right. I promise."

Horace couldn't see her eyes through the back of her yellow hair, but her words called out to him and told him where he'd knowed them same blue eyes. The courthouse. Her own granddaddy, the old Mr. himself, promising he'd keep Horace and Lawley and Willie Mae safe on they own land. The chain gang mens draped a log chain round his neck, this time so heavy he couldn't look up.

Greenback skittered toward the door. When he passed Horace, Horace lifted a heavy foot, and, knowing he'd have to stand by his own self this time, mashed the lizard flat. "Don't blame you none, old lizard."

Passing the yellow-haired girl and the blue police, he gathered up a chunk of rusted chain off the porch and drug it, creeping along in a slow moving slant, leaving a spotted trail of bright red pee. When he reached the split dogwood, Horace grasped the gray trunk, now grave with branches weighted heavy in Willie Mae's pink, buds waiting to open. Lowering his own self to the ground, he looped the rough chain round his old weary bones and Willie Mae Blesser's tree and snapped shut the lock.

# Childhood

"Stab the body and it heals but injure the heart and the wound lasts a lifetime." - Mineko Iwasaki

# Hard as a Rock

Imagine a stick-sized child, maybe five, with feathery brown hair. She wears a dress made from a standard McCall's pattern: puffed sleeves, gathered skirt, Peter Pan collar, and a bow tied in the back at her waist. She meanders about in the yard of her Aunt Macie's neighbor, Boots, waiting, while her mama visits inside.

This day, like any other Virginia summer day, begins cool and lightens late as if the sun has trouble climbing over the encircling mountains. It's warm, but not Alabama warm. It will cool again in the evening, and the little girl will don a sweater and nuzzle next to Aunt Macie until the two fall asleep.

A shallow river ropes around the block where clapboard houses sit on what appears to be a narrow jetty that juts into the river. Summer after summer of visits and the child accepts the stench of sewage and mud as natural. It is the only river she knows. She could crawl down the embankment to the water. She could wade and hop from rock to rock. She could watch tadpoles scamper and fish fight against the current. But she does not go there. Her grandpapa says if she gets back in the river, she will fall into a sinkhole and never come up. Or giant grey river rats will drag her under and eat her alive.

The little girl circles Boots' house. Nothing hints at a child's ever having been here. With nowhere else to go, she sits on a back wooden step and surveys the yard. Nothing to see but scant grass clumps and river rock stacked against the base of the fence to keep neighbors' animals from digging in.

Here at Aunt Macie's, over 500 miles away from Alabama, she has nothing to play with. At home she has dolls, puppies, and chickens. If she were home, she would scrape up some pine straw, stack it in flat, thin rows, and build a playhouse where she could sit in each area, room by room. She could envision tables, chairs, beds, tea services, mud pies, and baby dolls. But there are no pine trees. Nothing but an occasional maple tree and rocks. Smooth, round brown river rocks. Rocks the size of softballs.

As she sits, it comes to her. A row of rocks will make a sturdy wall. Boots has so many. She will not mind if she borrows a few.

It is decided. She will scoop up her dress like a sack, fill it with rocks, carry them down the block and across the street to build a playhouse in Aunt Macie's front yard. It may take several trips to get enough for a full house, but time is not a matter.

The first trip goes well. She dumps the rocks outside the fence at Aunt Macie's. Her grandpapa watches as he swings back and forth on the porch. He stops from time to time to spit his snuff into an empty tomato can.

On the second trip, the child realizes the rocks are rubbing dirt off on her dress. She brushes it off as best she can, but she can work again at getting the dirt off after she finishes her loads.

Between loads two and three, the child takes time to block out one room with a door that anticipates another room. No doubt, this playhouse will outshine any pine straw house anywhere. Her mama will not complain because copperheads cannot hide under these curved rocks like they do under straw.

Mama will be so proud.

Back for her third load, the child busies herself packing her skirt again. Boots' back screen door opens, and her mama demands to know what she is doing.

"I'm making a playhouse out of rocks. See. They're round. Snakes can't hide under them like pine straw." The little girl smiles.

"Put those rocks back," her mother demands. "Put them back right now."

"Leave her be, Margaret," says Boots. "It's just old river rock. There're plenty more. Let her have them."

"She's got no business bothering somebody else's stuff. Dump that skirt, girl." Her mama starts down Boots' steps.

The child drops the rocks and bends to put them back in place. Looking back to the two women, she says, "I'm sorry, Boots."

"No apology needed, child."

Margaret drags the child by her arm down the street. Her mother's face fires red when she sees the room the child has made. Her grandpapa swings and nods his head. Brown snuff smudges his gray beard like dirt.

"Go inside and get the belt," her mother says.

"I didn't take the rocks. I borrowed them. Boots said it was okay." The child walks backwards toward the porch trying to convince her mother she has not earned punishment.

When she steps up on the porch, she eyes her grandpapa, a silent question asking for help.

"'Spare the rod and spoil the child.' Proverbs 13:24," her grandfather answers. He pauses to spit.

Coming back with the leather strap dragging behind her, the child tries again. "I didn't steal the rocks, Papa. I was going to take them back."

"'Thou shalt not steal.' Exodus 20:15. That's what the good book says." He continues to swing.

"Don't sound like a good book to me. Not when it won't listen to the truth," she murmurs to herself.

Her grandfather stops the swing and leans forward as if he is about to tip out on the floor. "Blasphemy," he shouts. "Daughter. You remember the number. Five lashes. For defiling the Bible."

The child hands the belt to her mother.

"Hold that tree till I'm through," Margaret says.

By the third strike, the child has an imprint of bark pressed into her cheek. By the sixth, she weeps aloud. The little girl has pee dribbling down her legs, stinging the strips left by the belt.

Ten lashes and the mother stops. She lets the belt fall. "Change your underpants and take every one of those rocks back and apologize to Boots." Her mother sighs as if exhausted.

The child dries her face with her skirt. Streaks of dirt stripe her cheeks. She continues to cry from the pain in her legs and squats to dab at the sliced skin with her dress. She hiccups from loss of breath, but she fills her skirt again with rocks. She wipes her nose and face on her forearm.

At Boots' back door, the child struggles to hold her skirt with one hand while she knocks with the other.

Boots appears.

"I'm putting your rocks back, Boots. She says tell you I'm sorry I stole them. I won't do it again."

"It's okay, baby," Boots answers.

The child moves over to the fence base, bends forward at her waist, and begins to unload her skirt.

Behind her, Boots gasps. "Oh my God," she whispers.

The child tugs her skirt down in the back so Boots can no longer see the whelps and cuts that crisscross her legs.

She squats like a small calico hen, her dress draped over the ground, and begins placing the rocks in their original dents. One at a time.

From the back porch, Boots watches the child's labor.

The child returns with another skirt filled with rocks. She crouches into a small mound, her brown hair falling over her face and shoulders.

As mountain shadows move across the yard, Boots stands motionless. Chilled air settles over the valley. In the gathering darkness, Boots finds it more and more difficult to distinguish between river rock and Margaret's daughter.

# Fishtales Told to a Crow, Mid-Spring

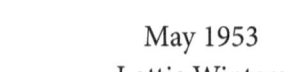

May 1953
Lottie Winters

Gary Evans drowned on Easter Sunday, but he didn't rise for thirteen days. When the water's still and the fish are tired, they grow roots to the bottom, long white roots, so they can stay in the same place as long as they want. I knowed this was true when Gary Evans drowned. Right here in Papa Johnson's pond.

Gary Evans stayed in the water almost two weeks growing to the bottom under black tree limbs. When the water started to warm up and move, his roots broke loose, and he come to the top all puffed like an adder and the color of mushrooms. His family kept the box closed to keep kids from poking at him to make the pond water run out.

I was born on Pest Hill, just out from Sandy Grove, where a long time ago they'd bring people with the pox to die in the big open house they called the Pest House. Going up Pest Hill you see right off a fancy white house with a yard pond out by the road. When I's a little girl at the Willington County fair, I throwed pennies and won a goldfish that glowed. I took my goldfish there to that yard pond so my brother wouldn't throw him down the toilet, and it growed to match the pond size. I put it there. But the mule pond where we fished ain't got fish that big, only Gary Evans for almost two weeks.

It's the pond in Papa Johnson's pasture where the mule stands against the heat. There's plenty of bream there, so I knowed Gary Evans'd go. He ain't much of a fisherman, so he likes a pond with plenty of fish.

At the pond, you can lay on your belly and look over the tall end bank. I still go there and watch the fish grow roots as the days warm up again. Where'd the fish come from, nobody knows, except maybe some science teacher at the school in town. Papa Johnson says he never put none in. No water in, no water out. Maybe crows drop them down from the sky.

The mule don't grow roots because his legs reach to the bottom in places where he shades. When he walks out of the water, his hoofs suck air out of the clay mud and leave bowls that fill up with water so tadpoles can grow legs and become frogs. And the fish eat the tadpoles. I've seen them do it myself.

Nobody knowed Gary Evans drowned on Easter Sunday but me, and I didn't tell. Just like I didn't tell about what happened after the fish fry and the sawmill last May. Jim Crow knowed what happened to Gary Evans, but he won't tell neither.

One time when I rode the old mule around in the pasture, I found this little crow, slick and shiny as a lump of coal. It'd fell out of its nest, so I brought it home and called it Jim. Jim Crow. Papa Johnson said he come to Sandy Grove when he was no more than a boy because it was a good Alabama town. A jim crow town. I figured he brought the jim crows with him when he moved from town so's they could live in his own pasture since he liked them so much.

One day when the road workers was working down under the hill, Jim Crow flew over to that oak yonder and set on that bottom limb. I seen it from the front yard and called him. "Jim! Jim!" And he answered back, whining up through his throat and out his beak, "What? What?" But he never flew back till almost dark. He stayed put, watching the strangers burying the ground under their shiny tar.

Jim Crow was there on the deep side of the pond when Gary Evans drowned. Gary Evans, born July 1930, drowned, 1953'll set long and hard on his headstone. Another month and it'll have been almost a year to the day after Papa Johnson's regular fish fry—when Gary Evans drowned.

Papa Johnson has the best fish frys in Willington County. Everybody's invited. Everybody comes. Bream season he'll set up black wash pots over open fires in the front yard, fill them with lard, and set the women to work. The men'll catch bream, some as broad as your hand, specially in May, and the women'll clean them. Scrape off the scales. Lop off the heads. Dip them in dry batter and fry them whole. If the grease's hot enough, they'll crunch up so's you can eat every bit. Fish and fins, fish and tail. All laid out on a loaf bread sandwich.

I knowed I wouldn't go to no more fish frys with Gary Evans there. First it's Christmas. Then winter's gone. Easter's coming round. Bream'd be biting, and the black pots set to be fired. I was ready.

The day he drowned I told Gary Evans I knowed about a pond off the side of the road with trees holding up the rock walls. Bream the size of a three-year-old. I told him I'd growed from last May when he took me from the fish fry to the sawmill to see where he worked. "I'm a woman now. Fourteen," I said.

I told him I had my daddy's liquor where I could get it easy, if he wanted to go to the pond with me. So he went with me, but I took him to the mule pond. He didn't know no different. When we got there, he was so sloppy drunk he wouldn't've cared if there weren't no pond at all. I knowed all

138

along he couldn't swim worth a lick, so he was going to be easy.

In the truck, it was the ride to the sawmill all over again. Him biting the inside of his bottom lip to keep back the grin told me he was remembering almost a year before, the same as me, but I didn't say nothing. I kept my face set.

## April 1952
## Charlotte Winters

Gary Evans watched Lottie play hide and seek with the younger kids, then he followed her out behind the smoke house where she'd squatted behind an old Rose of Sharon. "You're too old now for playing with these kids," he said. "Come on, Lottie girl. Come see my place at the sawmill. I got my own office now. I'll let you shift gears in my truck. Your sister won't care if you go. We're family now, ain't we? There ain't no difference in brother and brother-in-law but two words. Ain't that right? Besides we'll be right back. Come on, Lottie girl."

"My mama named me Charlotte, not Lottie."

"Sure. Okay. Whatever you say. Come on, now. That sawmill, it's a wondrous thing." He took Lottie's hand and walked her through the backyard, away from the house.

At the sawmill, he walked her around, showing her this, telling her that, 'til he'd led her out behind the sawdust pile. She looked up its sides. "Never seen nothing so big," she said. "Taller than the pasture trees," she said. She wanted to climb it, if she hadn't've wore a skirt.

"You just climb right on up," Gary Evans said. "It won't matter none."

She started trying to climb up the pile, when he stepped in front of her and slipped his hand under her blouse, grabbing her nipple.

"Good start for thirteen." He grinned.

"No." She kicked herself away and tried to run up the sawdust hill. It was like climbing a ladder with the rungs falling away under you, sliding down and groping around to hold on to something that's not there.

"Feisty little whelp." The satisfaction of her scare struck out through his eyes. He slapped off his belt, grabbed her legs. She was caught. He pulled her back down, then lifted her by the shoulders and stood her up in front of him so's he could look at her.

"I'll show you not to mess with Gary Evans," he said with his teeth in her face.

It was Lottie. It was Charlotte. It was Gary Evans splitting us in two. There on the sawdust pile. All we could hear was her panting. Her hands flat against his chest, her elbows straight as boards, she pushed away. He pulled her back to him. Her mouth gaped open. No sound coming out. Her eyes screamed words that wouldn't come out her mouth. He twisted both arms behind her, reached around in back of her, wrapped her wrists with the belt, and jerked it tight. He bent her head back and tried to pry open her mouth with his tongue and dingy teeth. Lottie's mouth wouldn't open.

"Trashy whore." He hit her hard in the belly with his fist. Her head drooped, then popped back, and she vomited up the bream and bread, fin and tail, out on to his shirt. It stunk. She stunk, like stale fish lard.

"Slut. You little bitch. I'll teach you not to puke on me." He looked toward the weeds. He was talking to hisself. "The crew and me, we spent all day poking at a little old chicken snake that come sneaking into the mill lot. If it ain't still alive, it's right here where we dropped it. In these weeds."

It was Lottie what went with Gary Evans to the saw-mill last spring, not me. My mama and daddy knows their Charlotte wouldn't go. Not for no man, no matter what he promised. But I can tell about it because I know the snake. The snake comes in my bed every time I smell dust in the night. My mama says it's just the folds in the covers, it ain't really no chicken snake, I'm the chicken. But he's magic. I know it. He disappears when Mama switches on the light.

And he's at the well. When I try to let the bucket down, gentle so I won't muddy the water, he's sliding down and down and down inside my hands. I can't bear to hold him no longer. I turn him loose because I can't stand the feel. Then the bucket thuds against the bottom and stirs up the mud that takes all day long to settle.

Lottie watched Gary Evans move toward the weeds. I saw her know what'd happen. She turned her head and saw the snake, brown plaid with a yellow belly. It was the biggest snake she'd ever seen, almost twice as long as she's tall. When she looked at the snake, something squeezed the breath out of her. She thought she might die and rot, her legs fixed there in the sawdust pile.

Gary Evans picked up the snake with both hands and stood in front of her in one move. The snake was spilling out of his hands. With his elbow, he pushed her down, then piled the fresh killed snake on her chest. She could feel the snake quiver as its weight hit her. Her eyes rolled back and she stretched her neck so she wouldn't have to see. She knew it would look at her and know about Gary Evans. The snake sucked out her breath and rooted her in the sawdust. It laid heavier on her than any man. As its ants crawled into her blouse, her shivers made them stumble across her body. She didn't dare move. Snakes don't die till sundown.

141

"Well, my little wall-eyed catfish, that ought to keep you still." He unzipped his pants.

Lottie squeezed her eyes shut. I looked up past the top of the pile and watched clouds float easy through the sky. Lottie and me, we heard him and him grunt like a wild boar. Then he fell into the sawdust by her feet and moaned. He lay still 'til his clumsy breathing stopped. Behind her lids, she could see her arms and legs as they laid where she would've put them, stone-still, like parts of a broken statue, separate from her body.

Lottie remembered what Papa Johnson had told her about snakes. Whip snakes put their tail in their mouth and roll after you, even up hills. She opened her eyes and watched Gary Evans roll over on his back and wipe his hands on the grass. He was chanting through his breath, "My love, my love, my Lottie, my love . . ." and staring off into the sky. She wanted to tell him he needed to be quiet so the snake's mate wouldn't come and pay back the killing, but the snake smothered her voice.

Then he stood up, kicked the snake off her, rolled her over with his shoe, and took his belt. She laid still, her face in the sawdust pile. "Just you wait, girl. You'll want old Gary one of these days. You got to get a little riper." He got into his truck and left her there, the snake wadded next to her in the sawdust.

When she heard him drive away, she kicked herself up and away from the snake, her heels sliding into the loose sawdust, her hands pulling her backwards. As she moved, her voice come back. Once it got back to her, it began to scream.

142

## May 1953
## Lottie

Fourteen now and old enough. I know about men and boys. I've gone to the high school in town for a whole year since the sawmill and Gary Evans. I hear the girls talk. It's all in the clothes, they say. And how you move when you walk.

So I put on some old tight blue jeans and rolled them up under my knees to show off my legs. I buttoned my brother's big shirt low and let it hang loose so's Gary Evans could guess what was under there and I set out early Easter Sunday morning.

I found him in the tool shed sorting fishing tackle. I told him I'd like to go fishing myself. He started to chew the inside of his bottom lip when I lifted my hair up off the back of my neck. I watched his muddy teeth through the crack in his mouth. "It sure's warm this morning," I said. "We could even go swimming. I know a pond with a shallow end."

I got into the truck he kept behind the barn. He slammed his door. I give him my daddy's bottle. He drove off. Down the road I told him, "Leave the truck here behind this pine stand and walk with me. I'll show you a fishing hole and a place with slick rocks that'll take us under for a swim when we walk on them, a hole under the bank where we can take off our clothes and play without nobody knowing, if we want to. It's real shallow there."

He'd drunk most of a whole bottle of Daddy's liquor going down the road, and he was wobbly.

"I'm older now and I know what a grown man wants," I told him. "Wouldn't it be too bad if this old shirt got all wet?" I pulled the shirt tight down across my breasts. I

143

remembered to smile and look out from under my eyes, like the girls at school said.

He grinned his truck grin again. This time it spread all over his face.

I led him out the pine stand, to the pasture, and under the wire fence. I kept him just a few steps behind my back, pulling him along with one hand to keep him from falling down, unbuttoning my shirt with the other one.

The mule saw us coming and moved back, under a tree where Jim Crow was waiting on a high branch, out of the way. As I'd tugged and he'd stumbled, I'd opened the shirt, one button at a time. When we got to the deep end of the pond where I watch the fish, I turned around and let the shirt fall down my shoulders. A breeze come out of Jim Crow's tree and run ripples across my chest. The air made my breasts stand up in front of Gary Evans. His mouth opened up wide, and greedy words come out of his eyes. He fell at me for a grab.

All I had do was step over one step, and he'd go straight into the pond.

But he didn't fall in. He stumbled against my chest and I fell, my head bouncing up off the ground. I didn't know 'bout the hit till I opened my eyes and thought to breathe again.

"You pushed me." I spoke through my teeth, while trying to dig my heels in the dirt to get up.

"Just getting you ready, Lottie girl." He laughed my daddy's liquor out of his mouth.

It was the sawmill all over again. Gary Evans was mashing me in the ground. And it was a snake, there on the ground. It had to be a snake, a firm thick snake, black with splotches all round.

A snake. Underneath my right side. I couldn't breathe.

"*Charlotte. Charlotte. Come here. Come here and know this for me.*" My voice yelled out, loud in my head.

Jim Crow said "What?"

"*Charlotte, you gotta be here for me.*" But Charlotte just stood there watching Gary Evans on top of me, mashing out my air. I looked up into the tree by the deep end of the pond so's I couldn't see his dingy teeth and squeezed my mouth shut to keep his spit from dripping in and choking me. I looked through the branches for Jim Crow. And I held my breath till I heard Charlotte answer me.

"*Don't be afraid, Lottie,*" she said. "*Remember the chicken snake. Remember its face. We saw it, you and me. At the sawmill. Look at its eyes. They look like the kitten in the barn. It can't hurt you again. Get up. Push it out of your lap.*"

"*Charlotte?*" I turned my head to see where her voice was. She was gone. I picked up the black spotted limb and hit Gary Evans in the ear. I hit and hit till he rolled off of my belly. I got up kicking and hitting, hitting and kicking, while he tried to wrap his elbows over his face. He didn't say nothing, just, "Grunt. Grunt. Grunt."

He tried to run, hunched over to break the whacks. Blood was all in his face, so he couldn't see what was before him. He run straight for the pond. He went in, a little dirt following him over the edge. In the water, stirring up mud in Papa Johnson's fish pond. He went under, into black trees, stiff near the bottom to hold him down, breaking the fish roots loose with his thrashing.

When he come back up, his mouth was open. His voice'd found its words. Shouting words left over from the sawmill. His hands grabbed at the air, trying to climb up and away from the water. But the air wouldn't take him, so after two tries, he settled down quiet into the pond.

The fish come near the surface to see who had caused the commotion and swum round and round till the ripples spread out on the bank.

The mule switched its tail to swat the flies. He lowered his head and looked off to one side. Jim Crow said "What? What?" but I didn't answer him. I just pulled the shirt up over my shoulders, turned round, and set my face to go back home.

# A Child Handed Down

Alma found the baby asleep under the back porch. Not yet two, it had crawled in during the night and nested in an old dent Harry's yard dogs had dug years ago. Using Harry's hoe handle, she nudged it gently until it woke and dragged itself out. Before lifting it and carrying it into the kitchen, she sized it up and down, wondering if this was what she'd been waiting for these years and just didn't know it. Twisting the yellow #2 pencil she wore in her hair like an errant twig, as if scratching out an answer to her own question, she whispered, "I God. Look at what we got here," then took it inside, bathed it off, and fed it hot oatmeal cooled down with cream.

Alma had first heard the baby cry just before daylight, but she put the blame on having early morning grogs or going through late change miseries. After all, she told herself, she was fifty-seven. Or maybe, she thought, hearing things comes natural, her being a widow living alone at the end of the road these years. Whatever the reason, the thought of a child of her own made her heart beat stronger.

During the day, she thought she'd hear whimpers, more whine than cry, like a puppy fenced off from its mama. She passed it off best as she could, but before nightfall, she searched out the sound.

"I'm Alma Tubbs. Harry's wife," Alma told the baby as she spooned in the mush. "No, better make that Harry's widow, little one." She shifted the baby in her lap. "Now, let's see. What's your name, you who dropped out of the nighttime sky?"

The baby stared at Alma out of heavy brown eyes and said, "MeMaw? See."

"I'm not your MeMaw, child. I ain't nobody's Me-Maw," Alma answered. "Fact is," she continued quietly, "I God. Ain't nobody's nothing, reckon." The baby nodded. "Bet you're all tuckered out, crying all night and half the day." So she made the baby a thick quilt pallet, wrapped it in her flannel pajama top, and settled the child on the floor next to the bed she'd last shared with Harry fifteen years ago. "Nice to have somebody else in the house, little girl," she said as she turned out the light.

The next morning Alma woke with the baby in bed with her. Curled in a ball, the baby fit beneath Alma's breast as if it was a part of her body Alma didn't recall. She reached down and rubbed the back of her fingers across the baby's cheek. "Soft," she murmured. "Soft as a young spring leaf." She smiled, convinced the child was a gift handed down from God. From that moment on the baby was hers.

At the time, Alma didn't know the Covington baby was missing. As soon as she turned on the radio, the announcer interrupted the morning swap-shop to say the county was looking for Mose Covington's step-girl, who, said Covington, wandered out of the house the night before. Though Sheriff agreed to lead the search, he hinted that he found it hard to believe that an eighteen-month-old child could open the door, walk out into the dark, and disappear without a trace. "Unless Mose had been a little more than drunk," he chuckled. "Everybody knows Mose's temper. He sure fire favors his liquor, specially when he gets to thinking about the little girl not being his own and all, and what with the baby's mother running off, leaving him to raise their own boy and her girl-bastard as well."

Alma didn't know, but she could guess. She didn't want to know about the Covingtons and their problems. Sounded like white trash to her, and one man's trash . . . so

148

they say. As far as she was concerned, the baby had come to her on her own, so the baby belonged to her. She didn't look too different from any other baby, so folk'd be easily satisfied.

Truth be known, this could've been Alma's own baby—if she'd been thirty years younger, and if she had not lost all her own back then. A young wife, she'd buried three babies out back of the barn. None come to term, each less than four months into her carrying, babies who'd plopped in a bloody clump into the bedside chamber pot, stark red against speckled blue enamel. She poured each one into a fruit jar, sealed the top tight, and buried it, each deep enough so coons couldn't ferret it out. She never told Harry about number three, since he broke most of her plates at the first one, then all her bowls at the second. After both times, grief drove him to sleep in the loft till weather drove him back in.

Morning of the baby's coming, as soon as she heard the car gearing down to make the hill, she ran to the window. She'd expected it. It was the law. She grabbed the Covington baby, a pillow, a blanket, and matches. She ran out the back, past the barn, and under the hill, down the steps into the storm pit. She lit the candle so the baby wouldn't have to know the dark again and put her on the blanket in the middle of the cement floor. Alma closed the door, flush against the ground. Before the sheriff parked his car, she had dropped cinder blocks on the door and pulled a downed bush over the opening. Harry had built the pit strong, strong enough to make it almost soundproof, so if the baby cried, the sheriff wouldn't hear.

She met the law at the front door and told him she didn't know nothing about a baby. Couldn't see how a baby could get to her place, seeing as how she lived in a hollow surrounded by a creek and heavy woods, all the time twisting the #2 pencil as if writing words on the back of her head, words a sheriff might find pleasing.

The sheriff thought the baby might've got lost and showed up here. The Covingtons lived through the woods behind her. Or didn't she know? And the creek was lower than usual this spring, without the rain. He stopped, staring at the pencil eraser sticking from behind Alma's right ear, then finished with his usual "and all." So frustrated with him ending everything he said the same way, she wanted to pull out her pencil and rub out what he said. But Alma let him talk, then showed him around, keeping her eyes away from the storm pit.

After he drove back up the hill, she lifted the baby out, and, holding it to her cheek, she promised on her soul that the baby'd never have to stay in the dark again. In the kitchen, she rocked her to sleep in Harry's old chair.

Within the month, Sheriff arrested Mose and charged him with murdering the Covington baby, though nobody'd found a body, as yet. The county farmed the baby's four-year-old half-brother Mark out to a woman up in Sipsey who raised kids for a living.

At the general merchandise, Alma let it be known in short chunks of sentences that her sister up North had a grandbaby she was too sick to raise, and she was going to Ohio to see what was what. She loaded the baby into her '54 Chevy and left at daybreak the day before Mose hung himself in the county jail.

Alma named the baby Dawn. In the fall, she brought her home and introduced her to folks, whenever necessary, as her own great niece from up around Cleveland. What people saw her praised Alma for taking on such a burden so late in life and urged her to move closer in. Alma stayed put. Never much of a mixer, she told Dawn.

Sheriff would come back to Alma's again, this time to question why Alma hadn't sent the child to school. He shouldn't need to ask. Any man could saw in her eyes that this old woman cherished this child beyond measure and feared losing her more than life itself. When he threatened to send the girl to a foster home up in Sipsey, Alma took her and put her in the first grade. For the whole year, three o'clock and the teacher opened the door to Alma waiting to take Dawn's hand. Dawn was eight.

Alma was looking at seventy when Dawn had her first real sickness. They'd gone through measles and colds and the pain of the curse without much ado, but this one was different.

Dawn drooped from place to place and had to be pushed to catch the bus for school. She had never liked school anyway, said the kids teased her because she was fourteen and in the seventh grade. But Alma saw things changing. Natural dark skin looked faded, no light in her hair, as if Dawn had been drained of life. She disappeared every morning before breakfast and refused to eat. Hot oatmeal cooled down with cream didn't phase her. Days all she wanted to do was sleep, and Alma sat by her bed, with Dawn turned to the wall.

In the second month of the sickness, Alma woke in the night and found Dawn gone, she called the sheriff to find her and bring her home. He had her back before daylight. Told Alma he'd found her and all. Back in through the woods. That's all she could get him to say.

It was then Alma knew Dawn was having a baby. Though she had never carried a child to full birthing herself, her instinct told her. When she told Dawn she knew, Dawn slammed out the back door and ran for the creek.

151

Alma let her go. She would be back. Dawn had grown up with the creek and the woods. That's where she spent most of her time these past dozen years. In the kitchen, moving back and forth in Harry's cane rocker, easy like a slow-gathering cloud, Alma scratched her head with the pencil and waited. Before sunset, Dawn walked in the kitchen door.

"MeMaw," she said hushed, "it's getting dark outside."

"I know it, Baby," Alma answered. She reached out her arms to draw Dawn in, but Dawn turned away.

Three weeks passed before Alma got Dawn to talk about the baby. Every night, Alma wandered through the rooms in her heart, searching for new people space in their lives, but she found none. Alma had filled each nook and cranny with her Dawn, with no space left. To squeeze two into one would pop her heart's old thin walls and spill blood out so far her face would flush crimson.

Dawn told Alma she meant to marry the baby's father. That he lived on his daddy's old place through the woods. Alma's heart stopped, sending a dagger-deep stab the length of her arm and out through her fingers. The only place through the woods was the Covington shack. Alma's right hand grabbed her left arm. It couldn't be the Covington place. God wouldn't do that to her. Besides, nobody lived there, had lived there all these years.

"Yes, they do. Mark lives there. He moved back last summer when he finished school. He's fixing it up for us and the baby," Dawn argued. "We want to get married. I need you to take me to town. To sign for me. Please, MeMaw."

"I won't," Alma shouted. "I God," she stammered. "I can't."

"Sure you can. Just take out your pencil and sign." Dawn smiled through the corner of her mouth. "I love him,

MeMaw." She looked so small standing before Alma, one hand resting on her flat little belly. "You can come visit. And play with the baby."

"You can't marry him." Alma's heart pounded, sending her breath out in little short gasps. "You don't know who he is." Alma clutched her throat to stop what she had almost said. "You don't know what you're talking about. Listen to your old MeMaw."

"You're not my mother." She bent toward Alma, her eyes on fire. "You can't tell me what to do," Dawn shouted.

"Don't yell at me, Girl. I may not be your mama, but I raised you." Hot anger shot through her veins and popped out her ears like a truck's backfire. "I didn't run off and leave you with no drunk, and I didn't let you wander off and get lost." Alma broke her words into quick runs with deep gulps between.

"What're you talking about?" Dawn's voice fell. "You said my mother died. You said my daddy was killed in the war. You showed me pictures." Dawn dropped to the kitchen floor and looked up at Alma. "What're you saying, MeMaw?"

She leaned over and pulled Dawn into her lap, cradling her baby's head on her shoulder. Boards unaccustomed to such weight in one place squeaked against the rocker. Heaviness the size of Jonah's whale pulled at Alma's arms. She recognized the smothering wet that lies in the belly of a fish larger than life itself, and she said, "You can't marry this boy, Baby Girl." She paused, and Dawn stepped out of her lap. Alma's memory whispered, *He's your blood kin*, but her mouth never said a word. Alma stopped the rocker. It was as if she'd been belched out on deserted sand, so desolate she felt at knowing she'd let the moment pass. Unsaid.

Starting the rocker back up, she took Dawn's wrists in her gnarled hands and lowered her child to eye level. "I

153

never said you's my flesh and blood. I told you your mama died because as far as anybody was concerned she might as well be dead, leaving you like she done. And your daddy could've died in the war. Nobody knowed who he was. I thought it best that he died in the war than hanging in some jail cell by his own bed sheet."

Releasing her grip on Dawn, Alma shook her head, fearing now she'd said too much. The #2 pencil jarred loose and hung in a slant toward her shoulder. Dawn reached out to catch it before it hit the floor. "We'll go north. Live with my sister for a spell, then come back, if you want. When you're over all this." Dawn didn't answer. "We'll give it away to somebody who'll love it."

Dawn drew her hand away from Alma's head and stepped back, bumping into the kitchen cabinet. She reached behind herself to stop her fall. "You don't understand. You're just an old woman. You don't know what love is." She looked at Alma and dropped to her knees, pulling out the drawer she'd grasped. "You never loved anybody in your whole life. Nobody but your own self."

Alma felt her face go white, like an over-bleached sheet. She whispered, "I don't know. I thought I did."

"How can you say that, MeMaw? I'll just die if you won't sign." Alma expected Dawn to stomp her foot like she usually did when in a tantrum, but she didn't. "I never had a family. Now I can have a whole family all my own and you're being so selfish you won't sign." She glared at Alma. Then dropped her head. "I'm going to have a baby, MeMaw," she wailed.

Ignoring the binding in her chest, Alma lifted herself out of the chair. The yellow #2 pencil slid to the floor and rolled into the far corner behind the table. Harry's rocker bumped empty on polished oak floorboards. She laid one hand on Dawn's dusky hair, the other on her own breast.

"Get up, Baby," she said.

Dawn jerked from under Alma's hand, and boosting herself up by the silverware drawer, she reached in and grabbed a butcher knife by its handle. She pulled it back, the point toward Alma.

Breath barely moving her bosom, Alma lifted her hand slowly toward her throat, leaving her chest open.

Dawn swiped the knife straight across the air between them, pricking Alma's arm. Seeing a strip of blood form on her mother, Dawn dropped the knife and sobbed, "Oh, Memaw, what have I done?"

"Nothing, Child. You ain't done nothing at all," Alma crooned. "I'm the blame," she said.

Dawn ran out the back door, clutching the knife before her. Alma followed her and found her crying in the storm pit, the slab door flung open to the sky. She lit a candle and sat down on the wooden bench, slipping her right arm around Dawn's waist. Dawn dropped the knife with a clink to the concrete floor. Between sobs, she said, "What're we going to do, MeMaw?"

Alma tried to lift her left arm to take out the pencil, but weight pinching her heart kept it from moving. "Go get the paper."

"We have to go to town," Dawn insisted. "The papers're in town. At the courthouse, MeMaw."

"You look just the same. The first time I saw you, Baby Girl," Alma's hand dropped open into her lap. Her words popped out in little skips and sweat wet her face. "Hurry up now. Before dark comes in."

# Martha Louise's Story

"April is the cruelest month . . ." - *The Waste Land* by T.S. Eliot

I'm not a liar. Few people believe me, but I swear by God's old dog that ever' word is fact. They say I misremember. I tell them sure as the stars come out at night this happened. And it happened to me—Martha Louise McClain.

It's 1947 and I'm six.

This Sunday afternoon we are visiting one of Daddy's hunting buddies, another dog man. Us girls play in the front yard. We wrestle and toss each other about on new grass and stain our shorts. We chase each other in hide and seek, ducking from one thick-trunked oak to another. Grown-ups drink sweet tea on the front stoop.

In the middle of a quiet spell, Daddy, from his place in the crooked wicker chair, looks to the east and sees a limp green sky, sky the color of celery left too long in the Frigidaire. He gets up and says, "It's time to go."

I beg to stay. I finally have the perfect hidey-hole deep inside a cluster of azalea bushes ready to bloom. But Daddy wastes no argument on me. We climb into our old black Ford truck, a 1940 clunker with a back window so small I can't look out and see what we've left behind.

Daddy steps on the starter, and we head for home. He fusses over the road. Not ten miles long, it winds back and forth, stretching the drive to half an hour. He makes the turn onto the riprap road that cuts through Mr. Hall's horse pasture. We pass a dense stand of limber pines growing down one side. Behind us, shadows darken the back window. Stringy, dark clouds block the light, ending the day early.

Something big is happening.

Intensity drives the car. Arteries stand out on Daddy's neck as he concentrates on getting my mother, my baby sister, and me home before the storm hits. Midway down the road, dust devils scrimmage around each other as if they all want the center spot.

Daddy bends forward in an attempt to see through the gray curtain of rain that has overtaken us. He strains against the wind, crouched over the steering wheel, not a word. My mother shushes me when I try to ask a question.

Then, a churning wind hits. Its strength slams into our truck. It lifts us and takes us across the ditch, across the fence and into the pasture, as sure as that tornado took Dorothy away from Kansas. Empty dog crates Daddy keeps roped to the truck bed fly over the cab. Splintered slats bounce off the hood like wooden rockets, then disappear into the wall of rain.

As quickly as the wind started, it stops. For a moment, we hang suspended in air—Daddy gripping the wheel, Mama's knuckles white around the door handle. The baby shrieks and slaps a fist against her ear. I sit on the seat edge, excited to see what else this great gust of wind holds. The truck never tips. Never turns. We are puppets, manipulated by some unseen hand stirring the air.

"Wow," I cry, "we're flying!"

My mother releases her grasp long enough to yank my braid and spit out a "Shut-up!" before pulling my little sister closer to her bosom.

The wind exhales and settles us in the horse pasture, atop tall grass now flattened by the passing rain.

Within minutes, rain reduces itself to a sprinkle. The wind lessens.

"Now!" Daddy pulls me out and plops me on his shoulders. "Before the wind comes back."

He slams the truck door. He never slams doors. Something I do not like has hold of him. Something bigger than wind.

Mama carries my sister close, her hand cupped over the back of the baby's head.

We don't get past the fence. On the other side, the ditch now overflows with gurgling water. Behind us, back winds rise. Mama and Daddy run back to the car, with my sister and me bounding and rebounding against their bodies like taunt metal springs.

Inside the truck cab, we wait. Our wet clothes steam when Daddy turns on the heater against the sudden temperature drop. Windows fog up in their fight against chilly outside air, an icy breath that trails the tornado.

"Be ready," Daddy says. "It'll be back."

I expect the wind to lift us again, to set us back over the fence, the ditch, and leave us upright on the road headed home. Instead, it rocks the truck back and forth like a cradle and moves on. We are left where the first wind put us—in the middle of the pasture, facing the wrong direction.

Outside the truck again, calm, cold air burns into our sleeveless shirts. I have lost my sandals, and wet weeds slide between my toes.

At the road, Daddy sets me over the fence, then across the ditch. I wait in the mud as he holds my sister to let Mama cross. Daddy sets me on his shoulders and holds tight to my ankles. We pad down the dirt road, its trenches now filled with dingy water. In the distance, we spot the creek, its location marked by smoky mist that climbs up its banks.

Where a narrow creek once ran, muddy water has scaled the banks to create a wide, gushing river. Trees poke out of the water. Bush tops sway with the swirl.

We have to cross the bridge to get to the Hall's house on the main road. I can't see where the bridge is. If we miss the bridge, we drop into deep water, deep enough to cover our heads and heavy enough to float us, like logs, down the creek.

Daddy walks to the edge of the water. I cling to his head, whimper, then cry. He squeezes my legs tighter. Mama tells me to hush.

He steps into what is now icy April water and shivers as he moves one foot forward. He steadies it. He steps forward with the other. Water inches higher up his legs, then past his belt, up his chest, and laps against my bare feet. My toes curl. I try to draw myself higher up my father's body.

"I'm freezing," I whine. "I wanna go back to the truck."

"Hush, Baby," he says.

The rising water shoots up and smacks my naked feet as we move forward. It stops under Daddy's arms. I feel him breathe deep when he steadies himself on a solid bottom. I look back.

Mama struggles against the water, holding my sister over her head. Mama has her hands under the baby's neck and butt for balance. Suspended in the cold air, my sister screams and flays about like a floppy rag doll. They fall farther and farther behind as Mama tries to follow a straight line behind Daddy.

Across the swollen creek, Daddy puts me down on the slick bank and wades back into the water. He returns with my baby sister in his arm, leading my crying mother by the hand.

Mr. Hall took us home. We had no barn. We had no toilet. We had no kitchen roof or door. Daddy nailed a tarpaulin where the door had been.

Later that night, I slipped past the tarpaulin. Hugging myself in my cotton nightgown, I looked up to see if the stars were still in place. There were all the stars, just as before, filling the black springtime sky.

# The Importance of an Education

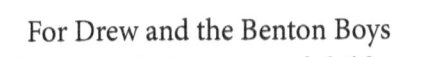

For Drew and the Benton Boys
who know the language of children.

Nobody ever asked why Travis called Roger "Gator Bait." Everybody thinks "That's just Travis for you." But Roger knows and Roger remembers.

It all started the summer before first grade. The idea that Grandpaw had been eaten by 'gators sent Roger reeling. Roger knows 'gators aren't in the river at all, or he thinks he does, but he took the bait and swallowed it whole when Uncle Lon dangled it in the barber shop. Travis just pulled him in, hook, line, and sinker. Or so Grandpaw says. That's Grandpaw's way of telling Roger he'd been duped.

The day he thought Grandpaw had been eaten, Roger was about to turn six. He had spent a hot July morning spooning out a dirt road for his truck. His mama, who was hanging wash on the line back of the house, sent him down the block and across the road into town to ask Uncle Lon when Grandpaw would be back from fishing Blue Creek.

Roger walks into a full shop. Doughbelly Mays sits propped back in the faded green barber chair. Mr. Doughbelly is getting his face softened for a shave, ignoring sweat running into his collar from the July heat and Uncle Lon's steamed towel. His white shirt and the white towel remind Roger of humps of yeast rolls rising in his mama's kitchen on Sunday mornings. Mr. Doughbelly is so covered up Roger wouldn't have recognized him without the glossy black church shoes he wears every day. Most men's shoes stay dusty in summer, not his.

161

Uncle Lon swishes his razor over the leather strop hanging from a hook on the chair, getting ready for Mr. Doughbelly's shave. Uncle Lon talks all day. "Don't see no point in yammerin' 'bout no ole Uncle Tom baseball player, no matter how good they say he is." Uncle Lon only cuts white men's hair. He doesn't let men from over Coal Hill come in his shop.

"Just might be interesting to see how he hits 'em balls," Preacher Black says. "But playing with them white boys? Where's he eat? Where's he sleep? Name's Aaron, say?"

Travis stands in front of the rotating fan, leaning against his broom. Leaning and mouthing off are what Travis does best. Travis is just that lazy. The fan kicks up more hair on octagonal tiles than the broom does. The hum of the fan buzzes through the shop like a slow moving bee.

Roger never has money. Travis does. Uncle Lon pays Travis, because he's eight now, almost nine, to sweep up the shop. Travis lets the fan do most of the sweeping. What the fan doesn't get, Travis pushes under the doormat when Uncle Lon turns his back.

"That's what the paper says. It don't say nothing 'bout nothing but his game, 'cept he's from down round Mobile. And he hits that ball like a hammer on a nail."

Uncle Lon glances in the mirror at Roger. "What're you doing down here, nephew?" Uncle Lon knows his sister doesn't like Roger to cross the road alone. He had spoken out again last week at Sunday table. Told Roger's mama she babies him too much. She's making him into a sissy.

"I'm not a sissy, Uncle Lon," Roger had said.

"Don't sass your uncle, Boy," Roger's daddy would have said, if he hadn't been way off in Milwaukee selling. He believes in Roger learning respect.

"Yeah, Squirt. What're you doing down here in my daddy's barber shop?" That's Travis. He can out-sass the best.

"Don't pick on your cousin, Son," Uncle Lon says. "Your Aunt Katherine don't want you hasslin' him." Travis turns his back on his daddy and looks at Roger, standing inside the screen door. Travis sticks out his tongue.

"Mama wants to know when Grandpaw'll be back from fishin', Uncle Lon." Roger looks away. Ignoring Travis' smart mouth is not easy.

"Why, hadn't you heard, Boy?" Uncle Lon says. "Grandpaw ain't coming back. Them Blue Creek 'gators done used him for bait. Blue Creek's full of hungry 'gators, waiting just under the water to grab old men and little boys who ain't in school yet." He swishes the razor again.

"My daddy says there ain't no 'gators round Copeland's Crossing. They're all off in Florida." Roger speaks quietly. He's not supposed to question his elders, but truth is he hasn't seen Grandpaw since breakfast.

"Well, figure it this way, Boy. Grandpaw ain't home, and he ain't here, so something must have done et him, and it must have been a big, fat 'gator. It's almost lunch time. He'd be back if he weren't et. My old man won't miss a meal." Uncle Lon laughs like Travis, mean and deep in his belly.

"Now, Lon," Preacher Black says softly. "Go easy there. He's a little 'un."

Roger's not sure if the preacher's teasing or not. What he says don't feel good either way. The preacher's words squeeze Roger's chest. He hears men down the line of chairs clear their throats. Some chuckle. Mr. Doughbelly's towel puffs up, then drops back down.

"He's eat up for sure," says Travis and nods toward the line of men like he's a member of the group.

Nobody moves. Roger hears his own breath. Short. Choppy. He's been looking at Uncle Lon's back, watching Uncle Lon watch him in the shop mirror. When Travis speaks, Roger looks at him against the wall, hanging on his broom, then down at the snippets of dark hair, scattered across the tile floor. The fan rotates into Roger's face. Its cool air whispers to Roger, telling him his face is red.

"Shore like to be a fly on the wall of the next game." Preacher Black folds the newspaper. "Where'd you see that baseball stuff, Lon?"

Uncle Lon says something about Roger's daddy up north, but the roar in Roger's ears won't let him make out the words.

Roger tries to swallow the choke in his throat so others won't hear, but it gets out anyway. It sounds like his puppy's whine when Roger stepped on its belly one night in the dark. He gets it. What Preacher Black said means he's either a little kid or dumb. Without raising his head, Roger says, "I ain't that little." He turns, pushes open the screen door, and runs. When he gets out of earshot, he calls back, "I'll show you. I'll show all of you."

Roger sits on the merry-go-round, still as a rock, his feet dangling above the rut cut in the dirt by decades of children pushing children. He stares at the corner wall where paint has curled and peeled off the overlapping boards from kids pulling at it during recess. He doesn't see Travis coming. He bats his eyes against crying again.

"Hey, Gator Bait. What's the matter?" Travis says. "Grandpaw's done home, and he caught a mess of catfish and he's ready to eat."

Startled, Roger spins around to face Travis. "Don't you sneak up on me, Travis Johnson." He stands to face Travis. "And don't you call me no Gator Bait."

164

"Cry baby," Travis laughs.

"I ain't no cry baby, neither."

"I seen you cry, Eegit."

Roger can't deny his red eyes, but he has his own weapon, one worthy of Travis' meanness. "'Sides, Grandpaw likes me better than you." Roger aims his words straight at Travis' heart.

"Ain't so." Travis puts both hands against Roger's chest and pushes him in the dirt.

"Is so. And you know it."

"Get up and say that again." Travis steps toward Roger.

"No. You'll hit me. You leave me alone, or I'll tell my mama."

"Ha," Travis replies. He walks away, toward Roger's house, ready to eat.

Roger murmurs to himself, "Anyway, Grandpaw lives with me. Not you." He pulls himself off the ground using the seat of the merry-go-round and heads home.

Roger had never liked the merry-go-round. Now, he hates it. Every time he sees it, he remembers Travis' words and Travis shoving him down. He can't go into the playground without seeing it in the middle of the back schoolyard. Its metal foundation, black against the white frame building, serves as the only playground for the children.

Some five years later, as a sixth-grader working at becoming a philosopher, Roger would decide, in the great scheme of things, that the merry-go-round had come first and the school had been built around it, as a precautionary defense. The building was much like a fort erected to ward off some unnamed enemy only the merry-go-round recognized.

Living next door to Copeland's Crossing School, Roger has known the merry-go-round as long as he can remember. It stands planted, the ground under it clean as a broom-swept yard, centered on a metal pole which lifts the seat almost two feet off the ground, just below Roger's waist.

Roger sees the merry-go-round as some sort of monster, the school building its protector, one an integral part of the other. The creature uses the auditorium to shield north winds. Two wings of classrooms jut out each end of the auditorium to buffet weather west and east. With its walled encampment, the merry-go-round sets immortal. Bought to be a simple piece of playground for younger children, the merry-go-round, over time, has taken on its own identity, fed by older students' need to dominate the schoolyard.

Children come to school expecting to learn to ride, unknowingly accepting their first ride as an initial rite of passage into the world of education. They step up to the merry-go-round and recklessly sling each other dizzy, each trying to whirl faster than the earth itself. For a first ride to be successful, it has to be solo. The rider must walk away on his own and keep his lunch down.

Older kids watch out auditorium windows as younger ones whirl. Sometimes when teachers have to keep a rowdy kid in for acting up, they send big kids out where younger kids play. Big-kid-bully locks in before little feet touch the ground. Their glee comes from spinning younger kids so fast little ones fly off, splat, in the dirt, and come up crying.

Roger knows the initiation routine. He has seen it happen, even before he started school; so, beginning first grade, Roger stays back out of the way. He tells himself he will learn to ride by himself. One day out of the blue, he'll jump on and spin himself faster than anyone has ever gone before. Flying faster than Superman. Kids'll stand back and stare, their mouths catching flies. He'll walk away without a blink or stagger.

On a cold Saturday, Roger tries to ride the merry-go-round for the first time. He'd just turned six. By mid-morning when temperatures rise above freezing, he turns off Howdy Doody and glances back to see that his mama hasn't noticed. He puts on a jacket, pulls down his cap's earflaps, and walks out the door. He tramps past the end of one school wing and into the merry-go-round's camp.

Before facing the merry-go-round, he has imagined himself taking the bar, running, pushing, then hopping on, sliding himself into the merry-go-round as smoothly as if the wooden seats are greased. He'll whirl so fast the bill of his cap will fold back, his hair will flatten out against his forehead, the wind's cold burning his eyes, tearing them, as it tries to scoop them out of their sockets. He has watched sixth-graders do this. Take the bar, run and push, then hop on and spin. For them it seems a wondrous thing, this being in charge.

Edging up to the merry-go-round, he looks around to see if anybody has followed him. Icy metal against his right palm reminds him he has forgotten his gloves. He can stand the shock. He has to be brave and ignore the cold.

He treks the beaten trench around the machine as chilly air smarts his face. Naked skin on cold metal glues his hand to the bar, pulling him forward as the merry-go-round gains speed. Roger's easy trot turns into a jog, the merry-go-round going so fast he can't jump on or let go. It's heavy. It's alive. Roger hadn't thought of this. Watching others from his place in the far corner of the playground, it had all looked so easy.

The machine controls his pace. Though he runs along side, the merry-go-round traps him with its spinning. If he drags his feet, it will stop. But he can't get his feet ahead of himself to plow them into dirt. If he digs his feet in, throws his body back, he'll slide forward. That'll make it stop. But his feet barely touch the ground.

Anger at himself for ever believing he could control this merry-go-round and hatred at the merry-go-round for placing itself in the middle of the school's playground now throw him into panic, and tears drop down his cheek. He knows he's trapped. If the machine doesn't stop, he'll pee his pants.

Caught and dragged by a mechanical toy, as surely as if some giant has thrown the cycle into motion, Roger whimpers, and a voice he doesn't recognize as his own whines, "Stop. Stop."

Behind him, Travis puts out one hand and stops the merry-go-round. Appearing out of the air itself, Travis leans into Roger's face and sing-songs, "Gator Bait's a cry baby. Wait'll I tell."

He kicks dirt at Roger and snickers as he walks around the building toward the ballpark on the other side of the sixth grade wing.

Roger has failed to ride the merry-go-round. Maybe Travis is right. Maybe he is a baby. Even the men at Uncle Lon's shop said so.

Roger doesn't try to ride the merry-go-round again. Not in front of other kids. And he can't trust Travis not to sneak up on him. At recess, he finds himself with two choices, play marbles in the dirt or build girly playhouses up by the plum bushes. Tubby Hambric plays with girls, but everybody knows he's a sissy. He wears trousers to school instead of overalls.

Travis would never leave that alone, not if he finds him in a pine straw playhouse. That's out. So Roger draws his circle and shoots his marbles.

Winter Saturdays with nobody around, he stands at the merry-go-round and rubs his hand over the frosty metal, fingering dents where paint has flaked away. During the week, he shoots marbles. Everybody else, even girls, rides the merry-go-round. He can't decide if he hates himself or if it's the merry-go-round's fault.

By mid-winter, and still a raw first grader, Roger decides again he has to teach himself. Alone, he climbs on the seat. Wearing gloves this time, he slides his legs under the metal bar and wraps his hands around it, facing the center, as he's seen kids do. He walks the merry-go-round with his feet, one foot crossing the other, each step increasing the speed. Seated with his feet inside the circle, he can stop or go as he chooses. Going is slow, but he goes.

He's watched at least two, sometimes three, bigger kids grab a bar and run the circle, taking the merry-go-round with them as they go. Then, as the merry-go-round takes on a life of its own, they throw the machine forward, stand back, and cheer on the riders. Riders stiffen their arms, lean back, girls' hair hanging loose, dragging in the dirt, and laugh, mouths open as they whiz by. If he challenges the merry-go-round every Saturday, he should be able to stay on, to be one of the gang, by spring.

March and Roger's had enough of side-stepping Travis. He's no good at marbles. Travis has all the kids calling him "Gator" now. He has to ride the merry-go-round, and he has to do it with other kids around.

He sees himself growing tall during the ride, stepping off bigger and stronger than moments before. He will not allow himself to be flung off and laughed at by Travis, who's big and strong and fast. Travis makes other kids call him "Sheriff." "I control this range," Travis says and slides imaginary pistols into imaginary hip holsters, just like Gene Autry.

"Gene Autry ain't no sheriff," Roger confronts Travis. Travis shoots his gun-finger at Roger and walks away.

The day for Roger's first ride comes within the week. Near the end of recess, Travis challenges Roger. "Ever'body's rode but you, Gator Bait. Still chicken?"

Travis' taunt draws other kids to the circle.

Roger steps toward the merry-go-round. "I can ride this ole thing," Roger announces. "It ain't nothing."

"Let's see how tough you are," Travis says. "I'll give you a ride myself. I won't sling you off. Promise."

Roger hesitates, then accepts that he can do this. Maybe Travis will keep his word. Taking the bar directly behind Roger, Travis starts slow. He trots along beside Roger. Roger breathes easier. *Yep. I can do this*, Roger tells himself again.

Without a word Travis speeds up. He runs along beside him then flings Roger into a dizziness that loosens his hands and sickens his stomach. Roger concentrates on not being flung off, never imagining the power of the merry-go-round would be so strong, stronger by far than the Saturday it got away from him in the fall. Faster than any of his practice runs. Faster even than Superman flies.

"Gator Bait. Gator Bait," Travis chants into Roger's left ear. The sing-song rhythm coincides with Travis' footfalls and Roger's heartbeat. Roger thinks "Hang on. Hang on." In the distance, he hears other kids join Travis, chanting "Gator Bait."

Roger leans over the iron bar, his head hanging forward, so the others can't see how scared he is. Behind him, he hears kids laugh, cheering him on. No. They're cheering Travis.

Roger manages the ride without crying out. When the ride finally stops, he stumbles, trying to get out of the iron bar that bound him. He wobbles over to the inside corner of the yard and vomits his lunch near the dirt circle where he shot his cats-eye earlier that morning, where he will eventually lose his favorite taw.

Pointing, Travis calls kids to gather round. "Look," he laughs. "Gator Bait's puking!"

When his heaves stop, Roger staggers sideways down the building and into the hallway without looking back. Throughout the first grade, every night after Roger goes to bed, Travis' guaranteed "Gator Bait" replays itself round and round in his head. Roger hears it in the rhythm of his step. He hears it when he runs. He hears it when he chews his food. The chant eats into his brain where his picture of himself hangs. Travis' beat bites off a chunk of Roger's image with each echo.

A few weeks after puking in the playground, Roger waits for dark in the side yard hammock. He's spent recesses since the day of the merry-go-round inside, volunteering to dust blackboards for teachers.

"He's so sweet," teachers say when he finishes. "He's such a dear."

"*Better a sweet deer, even a stuffed deer,*" Roger tells himself, "*Better even than a chicken.*"

He chews over his fate as white chalk dust covers his hands. He hangs different pictures of himself playing different sports, trying each on as if each is a new shirt. The images dangle across the back of his mind, waiting for Roger to decide on the right one.

171

He whacks erasers against the outside wall, creating a cloud of chalk. "One day I'll show 'em."

"What brought you out here by yourself, boy?"

Roger can sense Grandpaw eyeing him without looking up. He nods his head toward the plank building shielding the merry-go-round.

"I hate school. I want to go selling with Daddy."

"Let me tell you about that school sitting there." Grandpaw changes a subject to fit his need. He eases into the hammock by Roger. "That there school was built with the blessing of FDR, WPA, the preacher, and the town."

Roger looks at the roofline of the school beyond the plum bushes and wonders what a FDR and WPA are.

"Always been the heart of this community one way or 'tuther. 'Member takin your Grandmaw Sarie on a snipe hunt in them woods past center field on a night such as this. After I spun her silly on that ole merry-go-round. Not much left of them trees. Seems like school's growing out to take over the town. Or 'tuther way round."

"Third grade boys are pulling off loose paint again. On the back side. By the merry-go-round." Roger waits for Grandpaw to answer. He doesn't. "Travis helps 'em."

"Mad as fire, that's what he'll be. Principal'll clean their plow once he finds out. Don't you be into none of that business. You'll get took to the woodshed for shore."

"I don't scratch the paint." Roger pauses, thinking long and hard. Don't say this, he thinks. But his next words sprout from his mouth on their own.

"Do you think I could play baseball? Mama says I can't. Maybe she'd change her mind if you say so. When Daddy was last home, he told me about seeing Hank Aaron play baseball in Milwaukee. He said he'd take me one day. Hank Aaron's a Brave."

172

"To watch some Uncle Tom hit a ball? I'd say not. Ain't nothing brave 'bout hitting or throwing a ball." Grandpaw rocks quiet for a moment, then starts up again. "Pick a ball you can get your hands on and aim for dead center. Hit that ring. That's what basketball's about."

"You get pushed down in basketball."

"You get back up. Why, I recollect myself being in that old school. And the auditorium. So big it stayed cold, even with four wood stoves going. Seen many a day, that auditorium. Box suppers, political rallies, Halloween carnivals. I courted your Grandmaw in that very auditorium. And basketball games. Them was the best."

"Mama says I should play basketball, but I want to play baseball." Roger tried not to whine. "They have pictures in the paper. Kids look up to baseball players." Roger wanted to add "And they don't call them sissy names."

Grandpaw doesn't answer.

"Hank Aaron's on the All-Star team. I could be an all-star player."

"Tell you my ninth-grade team come this close to winning a trophy?" Grandpaw measures the missed championship as a half an inch with his thumb and forefinger. "When you're bigger, you can play basketball."

"I want to play baseball, Grandpaw. Center field. I wanna throw."

"Stick with basketball, if you ask me. End of every season there'd be a banquet. Tables set down the middle, white wood folding chairs, so slick with paint you'll nigh slide off in the floor, and the whole team church-quiet in dress shirts, bowties, and shoes, spit-polished till you see yourself in the toe."

"Like Mr. Doughbelly?"

"Now didn't we look just fine. I can see it like yester-

173

day. That's when I first set my sights on your Grandmaw. I tell you that?"

"But I want to play baseball. All the boys play baseball. Even ole Travis is going to play baseball."

"Wood heater set the floor on fire and burned the church to the ground the year you was borned. '50? '51? Held our sermons in that same auditorium 'til we men finished the new church. That auditorium belongs to the school. Building belongs to the state of Alabama. That's what politicians say. They don't know nothing. School itself, it's your mama and daddy and you and me. That's the way it's supposed to be."

Grandpaw sidles away, leaving Roger alone in the hammock. Loneliness overwhelms him. It's always this way with grown-ups. They never hear what you say. Even when they're not deaf yet.

One July Saturday, Roger finds his mother and Travis' mother, his Aunt June, at the kitchen table, his mother sorting fruit jar lids for summer canning. Summer's going to be gone, and Roger hasn't tried to ride the merry-go-round since Travis made everybody laugh at him for puking last winter. He's got to find something to be good at so kids won't laugh when he walks by. He can't face second grade with kids calling him Gator. Roger'd bet his cap pistol some kids don't even know his real name.

Roger has been thinking hard about playing baseball since he heard about Hank Aaron. The image of himself in a uniform, standing in high out-field grass, sets well with him. "Mama," Roger begins. "About baseball, I'm bigger now and . . ."

"Don't start that again. You're not old enough. Give it a few more years," she says. "Go watch television. Your daddy didn't buy that big twelve-inch screen to catch dust."

Instead, Roger pulls up a kitchen chair.

Aunt June leans out over the table on her elbows. She blows her saucer coffee, then sips, returning the saucer to a level in both her hands. Saturday morning coffee and cigarettes in his mama's kitchen, the two of them planning Sunday dinner. That's the routine.

"Now you take my Travis, Katherine. He's going to play baseball even though he'll only be in the fourth grade. I don't worry none because he's big for his age, going on ten." She slurps the coffee.

Roger's mother looks up from the jar rings and smiles out of the side of her mouth at her sister-in-law. "Roger's just coming up on seven," she replies.

"And I'm big, too," Roger counters. His spine stiffens when people talk about him like he's not there.

"Lon and me, we give our boy chances to shine." She blows the coffee again, causing little ripples to run for the edge. "You're going to have to let loose of Roger one of these days, or he'll never develop them social skills like my Travis." She sips again.

"Roger's fine just like he is. No need for him to try to be anybody but himself, June. If he plays ball, he can play basketball like his Grandpaw did." Mama rattles metal jar rings. "He won't mind playing a sport where he's less likely to get hit in the head. Being like Grandpaw won't be so bad." She turns to Roger and smiles, "Now is it, son?"

She speaks to Aunt June, "He'll just have to grow a little taller, that's all."

Travis knows Roger wants to play baseball. "You got to do something, Gator Bait. Else nobody's ever gonna choose you for nothing. Gonna to be a runt all your life. Huh?" He hits Roger's shoulder. "Huh?"

After a winter of playing by himself and this past spring feeling sap rise in his veins, as Grandpaw says, Roger decides he's fed up with Travis. He's fed up with Travis chanting nightmares in his sleep. He's stomping-his-foot fed up. He's ready to do something that says "Here I am. I am Roger Sanders. Not Travis' little cousin. Not Gator Bait." Roger answers Travis. "I'm gonna play baseball for the Braves. I'm gonna to learn to pitch long balls. Hard balls. I'll get a strike ever time I throw."

"Yeah? Like you throw up when you ride the merry-go-round?"

An argument can wait. "I can do whatever I want," Roger says. "I'm going to be just like Hank Aaron."

Sundays Travis' family takes noonday dinner at Roger's. Nothing ever changes. His mama and Aunt June come straight from church and fill the dining room table.

Grandpaw eats in his bedroom. "Too many big dogs in the smoke house to my liking. Just keep to myself this go round." Every Sunday he says the same thing before he fills his plate, goes upstairs, and sleeps off his meal.

Aunt June frowns. "He ain't never had no manners."

Uncle Lon soothes her. "It don't matter none. The ole man talks in circles anyway."

After Roger's mother has cleared away the table and gone into the kitchen, Travis blurts out to the men waiting for Aunt June's pound cake. "Roger wants to play baseball."

Roger doesn't say a word. With Grandpaw upstairs, nobody's there to defend him. After what Grandpaw said about loving basketball the night of the hammock, Roger isn't sure even Grandpaw'll take his side.

Roger eyes Travis across the table as Aunt June sets down saucers of cake.

Travis talks about what a good season the team will have. "Coach says I'll be real good by fifth grade. I bet I'll hit winning homeruns."

"Now don't you puff yourself up too much, Sonny Boy," Uncle Lon says. "What'll be'll be." He cuts a slice of Aunt June's pound cake into fourths and stabs one section, waving it in the air. "Just wait and see. You boys go on out back and throw a few. Or run down to the school yard and have a few spins on that old merry-go-round. Nothing like a good ride on a Sunday afternoon."

"Remember the day I slung you off the merry-go-round, June Bug? Eighth grade it was. Barefoot weather and hot as dickens. The way you yelled, you'd've thought I come within an inch of killing you. Landed right smack dab in the dirt. I picked you up and dusted you off. Knew then and there I'd marry you. Tears and all." He slaps Aunt June on her bottom.

"Not in front of the boys, Lonnie," she giggles. She leaves Uncle Lon and Roger's father, home from selling, to finish the cake. "Katherine can use some help in the kitchen."

Roger leaves with Uncle Lon talking to his daddy. "Now, Brother-in-law, 'bout niggers playing long side white boys up north."

Once outside, Roger glares at Travis. "I'm not going down there with you."

"Chicken," Travis replies. He bends his elbows, hooking his thumbs in his armpits and dances around Roger, flapping make-believe wings against his ribcage. "Cluck. Cluck, cluck."

"Mama told me not to." Roger lies, turning in a circle to avoid having Travis in his face.

Travis snorts and runs, calling back over his shoulder. "Gator Bait's a wimp."

Roger stands in the yard for what seems like forever, looking down the hill at the merry-go-round, then goes to swing in the hammock. He's not sure he ever wants to learn to ride that old merry-go-round.

In late August with Roger's second grade about to start, Travis crosses his heart. Hopes to die even. "I'll leave you alone. I swear. I double-dog swear. Just go to the store for Mama's cigarettes. She's your aunt. You ought to do something for your only aunt." Lying in Grandpaw Johnson's hammock, Travis pushes himself off with his foot and sways back and forth.

"Why can't you go? She's your mother. She told you," Roger argues. The sun burns hot, toasting grass and wilting leaves. Roger wants to be left alone. His daddy told him about watching Hank Aaron play again and being named the National League Most Valuable Player Award. He wants to think about baseball. And seeing Hank Aaron play.

"If you go, I'll meet you out behind the school and teach you how to throw a ball so when your mama says you can play baseball you'll be ready."

"You're creepy," Roger says and edges away. Learning to throw baseball is one thing. Trusting Travis is something else again. "I don't believe you."

"You want to be stuck with some girlie game like basketball?"

"Grandpaw played basketball. He's not girlie." Roger insists, "'Sides, why don't you go? Aunt June told you, not me."

"I got important things to do. Things a kid like you wouldn't understand." Travis rolls his tongue around and spits, as if he has a wad of tobacco in his cheek. "Do you want me to pitch to you or not?"

Roger sees a picture of himself in school red and grey, a massive catching glove on his right hand, and blocks out Travis as Travis rises and dumps himself on the ground. Maybe if he triple-dog swore. He's my cousin. I got nobody else to teach me. Grandpaw's too old. And he don't know how.

Roger agrees.

A dirt road runs behind the school's backstop Grandpaw built by stretching chicken wire between two-by-fours and down third base line. Boys have cut a footpath from the baseline, through blackberries, Preacher's yard, to the back of the store.

As Roger walks by the backstop, he spots himself out in center field, a dot where the trees shape a V, standing in grass that covers his shoes and brushes his calf. The ball will fall out of the sun and, whomp, smack into his glove. He'll fire the ball steady, solid like Travis throws the merry-go-round. He'll never miss, his throw true every time. No batter will be safe from him.

Always right on when he comes up to bat, he'll knock the ball into the pines and round second within the blink of an eye. Third base coach flags him not to brake at the bag, to head straight for home. The crowd on the hill stands and cheers. The team swarms and pats him on the back. Travis'll come to practice the next day and Coach will say, "Sorry, Travis, but Roger bumped you clean off the team. Maybe next year. If you improve."

Grandpaw in his folding lawn chair will sit on the hill near first base, just under the sixth-grade windows. He'll jump up and yell, "That's my boy out there." Grandpaw watches Travis play, but he never jumps up to yell.

Roger likes to think that, even though Travis is his only first cousin and even though Travis lives next door, Grandpaw will always choose Roger over Travis, no matter what. When he moved into town, Grandpaw could have lived with Uncle Lon or Roger's mama Katherine, and he chose Katherine, his "Kate." He's heard his mama say the reason is Aunt June. She snaps at Uncle Lon about Grandpaw, though he don't even live at her house.

"That woman, when she gets to heaven, she'll ask to see the upstairs," Grandpaw tells Roger. "Never satisfied with the way things are. Unless it's that durn boy Travis."

Roger tells himself, "If Grandpaw don't like Travis, I might not have to learn to ride the merry-go-round after all. Ever thing'll all fall in place. I'll learn to play baseball just like I'll graduate ninth grade, then ride a bus to County High. Mama and Daddy did, just like Grandpaw did. It's my legacy, Grandpaw says. Says I've earned it."

Roger brings Aunt June's Camel cigarettes to the back of the school and sets the paper sack down on the step, next to Travis' foot.

"Now can we pitch some balls."

Travis doesn't answer.

"Travis?"

"Only if you ride the merry-go-round."

Roger looks square into Travis' face. He never noticed that Travis' eyes are set almost on top of each other, with hardly no space for a nose between. Just like an old snake.

A blaze burns inside Roger. "That's not what you said. You crossed your heart," Roger sputters. He feels himself getting madder and madder at Travis, his face getting hotter and hotter. "You even made a double-dog swear. You promised me."

Roger knows in his heart of hearts the merry-go round won't stop this time at making him puke like some old dog. If he gets on it again, it'll send him flying off its plank seat and whirling into space. He'll be lost somewhere between earth and Superman's planet. Nobody will ever hear from him again. He'll just disappear. Eaten up by the air.

Travis'll never tell what happened to him. Roger'll never see Grandpaw again. It'll be like he was eat by 'gators and Grandpaw'll spend the rest of his life feeling like Roger felt that day last summer at the barber shop. A load sitting so heavy in his stomach that it drags his feet.

"You scared, cry baby? You're too puny to even be 'gator bait. Everybody knows a ball player ain't scared of nothing. Not no sissy merry-go-round. Still chicken. Cluck. Cluck. Cluck." Travis sounds like an old hen afraid the house-dog is out to steal her biddies. "Daddy's right. You're just an ole whiny butt."

Roger looks at the merry-go-round. It sits in the center of its own shallow ditch without moving. He looks at Travis. Travis bites his bottom lip, like he's holding in a giggle. What Grandpaw told him one night in the hammock moves him toward the merry-go-round. "Do what you're told, and you'll stay out of trouble." Roger had thought he was talking about grown-ups, but was he talking about Travis, too?

He carries his feet, one step at a time, across the play-ground and climbs on, wrapping one leg around a bar bolted to the seat. He sits down, then winds both arms around the bar, pulling his chest against the metal. He squeezes his eyes shut and holds his breath. If he don't breathe, he can hold himself inside his body, and if his body is locked to the mer-ry-go-round, he'll stay in the school yard. He'll not fly off into the sky and disappear.

181

Travis grabs the bar behind Roger and runs the circle. He flings Roger into a spin then stands in one spot, catching the bar behind Roger each time it comes by, pushing faster and faster. Travis is practiced at throwing, and he throws hard. Each time Roger spins past, Travis chants louder and louder, "Gator Bait. Gator Bait. Gator Bait."

Roger's upper arms begin to burn from clenching the rounded bar. He waits for the metal to pierce his skin and hook into him like a caught fish. He looks at the sky to focus on a cloud, a passing bird, anything to hold him in place, but the sky whirls by so fast all he sees is the roofline of the school, a fake line that blinks each time he cycles past the building and into the open. His lunch wiggles inside his gut. Roger clinches his jaws to keep it down.

"Travis? You down there?" It's Aunt June. "Where's my Camels? I told you to go to the store. I ain't going to pay some boy when he ain't done his job. If my cigarettes ain't here in exactly three minutes, you won't get this nickel."

"I got them. I'm coming." Travis sticks out his hand, grabs a bar, and braces his knees to stop the merry-go-round as Roger comes by.

Roger drops his head over the bar and rests against his arms.

Travis speaks from what seems to be somewhere far off. "See you later, Gator Bait." He laughs. "Wait'll I tell Gator Bait couldn't make it off the merry-go-round." Travis walks toward the sack and his mother's voice.

Roger steps out of the merry-go-round. He stands in one spot with his hand behind him on the seat, using the merry-go-round for balance. Steadying himself long enough to stop his head from whirling, he looks down to help set his head and stop the tears he feels rise with the vomit in his throat. He turns his back on Travis and faces the auditorium so Aunt June won't see him cry and tell his mama he's a baby.

Behind him, Roger hears the paper sack with the cigarettes crumple when Travis picks it up. Travis laughs again. "Gonna puke in your marble circle again, Gator Bait?"

Roger whirls around. Travis swaggers like a TV cowboy toward the corner of the school with the sack of Aunt June's cigarettes in his hand. "Travis, you . . . you stupid block head," Roger stammers. "You better leave me alone."

Travis doesn't turn around.

"You better listen to me, Travis Johnson, or you'll be sorry."

Travis laughs and keeps on walking.

Something Roger has never felt before rises inside him. He forgets his dizziness. He swallows hard, repositioning his lunch. He needs to hit something. To hit something with all his might.

Roger stumbles over to the school building and picks up a fist-sized brick that has been pushed out of the school's foundation by age and the wall's weight. An old orange chunk of brick, all corners, no rounds. It has gray mortar stuck to one side. He tests it with a slight up and down toss. Yep. This is the right one.

Roger lifts his right arm, his center field arm, straightens his elbow, and rotates the brick in a wide arc. He's seen the sixth grade pitcher do that, just before a strike out. The way he imagines Hank Aaron might ready a throw. He eyes the direction as if it's his cats-eye and winds up. He fires the brick with all his might at the back of Travis' head.

Travis drops with a thud to the ground.

Aunt June's cigarettes never spill out of the sack. Roger sees Aunt June coming. She'll have a fit when she sees Travis flat on the ground, a bloody spot already coloring the back of his flattop. Roger stands immobile, the merry-go-round separating him from Travis.

Travis crawls up on his knees. When he sees Aunt June coming, he whines, "Roger hit me. With a rock." He puts his hand to the back of his head. "Mama, I'm bleeding." He starts wailing so loud Uncle Lon can hear him at the barbershop.

"My God. My baby's bleeding. What on earth have you done, Roger Sanders?" She doesn't look at Roger or try to pick Travis up. She runs back toward town, bent forward, her head trying to beat her legs up the hill, yelling all the time. "Lon. Lon-n-n-ie. Katherine. Come down here."

Roger slaps school dirt off his hands. Hank Aaron would be proud.

He doesn't wait for Travis to get up. He ambles round the sixth-grade hall toward the baseball field and trots down the incline where Grandpaw sits to watch the baseball games. When he sees center field grass, he breaks and runs.

He doesn't need to learn to ride the merry-go-round. He's past that. Grandpaw was right. He done what he was asked. He stood up for himself. He don't need Travis. Today he pitched a straight, hard ball. He made his mark. That's all he needs to know.

Now powered to fly, Roger runs the bases. He toes each one, leaning in toward the pitcher's mound. Roger kicks up a rooster tail of dust high as Mr. Doughbelly's gut and heads straight for home plate.

# The Last Time an Angel Passed

I have been told time and again how I came to lie with my mama in her coffin. For years, we had the picture my aunt made with Daddy's black box camera to prove it.

It was May. I was three months old. Mama's pine coffin lay on two sawhorses in front of the empty stone fireplace. She wore a pink button-up dress with a white lace collar. Her lips were dark from dewberry juice and swollen by venom.

In the cool of early morning, she had reached into sprawling briars for a thumb-sized dewberry. That's where he struck her, on her left hand. Then he kissed her lips, this thick-bodied rattler, so swift she never saw him move. She screamed, clutched her left hand to her bosom, and ran. She died before the sun set.

Before noon the next day, children chased each other, boys wielding sticks and hissing as they ran doggedly after girls who squealed like terrified piglets. Kitchen women stepped on each other and cussed the heat as they warmed food for the mourners. At the barn, men cut and nailed the box. Once finished, they stayed put, sipping whiskey and smoking rolled cigarettes.

In the parlor, Daddy jiggled me. He paced the floor. "Shhh. Shhh," he said.

"Let me soothe her," Aunt Millie said.

Daddy ignored her and continued to walk the floor.

"Maybe she's wet." Aunt Millie followed him back and forth.

"Shhh." He paused before the open coffin and looked at my mama. He lifted her puffy, purple arm and tucked me into the arc.

"Willard?" Aunt Millie whispered.

Stillness quieted me, and I slept.

Daddy stepped away, his hands outstretched, palms toward the floor. "Now." He patted the air with both hands, as if he were sowing a seed. "Leave her be." He stared at me and mama, stock-still.

"It's time, Willard," Aunt Millie said. "Take the baby." He didn't move. She clicked the camera's shutter. He flinched and stepped outside. "He'll be back," she said.

The green metal clock struck four. I cried out. Daddy slammed the screen door and stumbled against the narrow end of the coffin. "Who put this baby in this coffin?" he said. His weight pushed the box into the stone chimney. The head slid toward the center of the room. Aunt Millie dived in from afternoon shadows to catch me as the coffin tipped toward the floor.

"Who left her to cry for her mama?" he said.

"You did, Willard." Aunt Millie lifted me away from my mama's body. She sat on the floor with me sheltered in her arms.

For a second, nothing moved. Those that knew such would say that was the last time an angel passed over our house.

Kitchen women rushed in to lower Mama's lids and resettled her in her coffin. One called for a man to nail down the top.

Still on the floor, Aunt Millie spoke to me. "Here, now," she said and unbuttoned her dress.

I rooted around, searching for her nipple. She pulled her breast to my face, and I suckled myself to peace. Daddy went back to the men.

Before the burying, a kitchen woman decided to send me home with Aunt Millie and my two-month-old cousin Jake. At dusk, a cluster of sweaty bodies trailed the coffin up the knoll and covered my mama with dirt to save her from the heat. By mid-August, Aunt Millie's husband, Daddy's brother, Uncle, would lie on the same hill. He caught Elbert Newsom's rabid dog in his chicken coop. The hefty hound chewed him up bad when he tried to get it out. Uncle couldn't live past that.

Daddy moved me, Jake, and Aunt Millie back to the house built around the sooty rock fireplace. He placed the picture Aunt Millie had taken of me and mama in the center of the mantel. There it stayed.

I would come to call my aunt "Ma" and Jake "Brother."

Mornings Daddy straightens the picture of me nestled under my dead mama's arm. He mumbles to my mama's picture, "It's Biblical." He adjusts it again. "Ruth and Boaz," he says and leaves for the barn.

Nights I can't sleep easy. Photographs follow me to bed. Mama with her own mama and daddy. Mama a girl by herself. As a young woman. Mama and Daddy the day they married. Mama and me in the coffin.

In time, I ask Daddy why not Ma. He says, "Leave it be." But I see the gloom in Ma's eyes when she passes the mantel. I see it when she sneaks off to sit by Uncle's grave. And it's there when Daddy takes Jake out back for a strapping. I never see Ma cry, but tears behind her eyes keep daylight out of her face.

A bitter January night. A raging fire. Daddy with his animals. Jake tending his ponies. Ma in the kitchen soaking clothes on the stove. It's time I rescue Ma from the shadows. I lift the center frame and take out the faded photograph. It's as risky as separating an egg. I drop Mama and me on the fire. We curl and blacken.

The back door slams. I grab into the heat for the photograph, but a suck of wind draws us up the chimney. One swallow and the image is gone. I nudge the empty frame back a bit so nobody will notice that what was has vanished. Mama's prints inch across the mantel, all strung out like decorations on an altar.

I crawl into bed and wait for sleep. Again, dark brings with it oversized dewberries and brown and gray rattlers hiding in wooden coffins. But tonight's different. I close my eyes and the coffin explodes. Rattlers spill over the sides. Red flames morph into orange, their centers scorching blue-white heat. Logs in the next room sizzle.

I cover my head and wait for morning.

# Boogollies, Lace Curtains, and a
# Dog in the House

### The Stallworth House

Fifteen miles from town, the old Stallworth house marks the hilltop. A red cedar, tall as the house itself, once stood in the corner of the front yard. As a child, when emotions consumed her, Hannah sent her own knowing self into its branches, heavy with steel-colored tips.

Twenty years ago, the 1966 tornado took out the barn and most of the tree, leaving only a ragged trunk. And the house, it left untouched. Three years later, a new owner brought in hay for wintering his black angus and stacked rectangular bales, barn-style, in the two downstairs front rooms.

Hannah parks her silver Cherokee jeep, and, checking the rearview mirror, pats foundation on her upper lip to cover the scar. She brushes cropped hair back from her forehead with her fingers, then climbs through the barbed wire fence, careful not to snag her linen slacks. Moving across the yard, she edges past dark-tongued beeves. She steps among thick, rancid paddies where she once played with her pup, a chow chow, his auburn fur soft as dandelion fluff against her cheek. She walks toward the house, around Black Angus, so rooted to the ground they seem to have entrenched themselves in the land even before man walked this hill country.

The house has never been a prosperous house. It is instead a severe house, one with forgotten dignity, yet worthy of a name. Had Hannah given it one, her choice would have negated the embarrassment of its drooping roofline, its shame at having hay bales piled across the porch blocking light into windows where her mother had entertained behind a lace curtain, bleached white and impeccably ironed, its intricate pattern willowing against worn wooden walls.

Dingy clapboards, never having been painted, bow away from nails, forcing rusty heads out of the wood. Irregular foundation rocks have allowed spaces between three tree trunks used as columns to sag so much the porch roof swags in broad scallops. Warped pine boards replace thick river rocks leading to the porch. Easier for hauling in hay, Hannah reasons the current owner might have thought. She tests the wood with her foot before moving on to the porch. At the far end, missing boards expose musky foundation dirt where the yard dog once slept flattened out against summer heat.

She steps inside. Korean War newspapers, nailed over wall cracks to block wind coming up the hill, hang in narrow bands. Two front rooms, bedrooms, both open to the porch. With ceilings at no more than six feet, it is as if the one long attic room above weighs so heavy that its floor presses against the bedrooms below, squeezing out the air. After one visit spent bending their heads sideways, lanky people didn't come back. Or if they did, they stayed outside. Water stains streak the inside kitchen ell where age and instability of the tacked-on room pulls its roof away from the house. The kitchen floor, once blue linoleum splotched gray, slants downhill.

Drop a saucer and watch it roll, like a marble, toward the back door.

"Hannah? What's that clanking?" her mother calls. "That better not be my good dishes."

But it was.

It is a simple house, these three rooms, unused attic, and a wide front porch. The long attic atop the two bedrooms creates a house as tall as it is long. From a distance, a passerby would swear a heavy wind could topple it.

As a child, Hannah would run from the back stoop, into the kitchen, through her parents' bedroom, and out the front door, all in one easy line, her feet barely touching the floor.

"Don't slam that screen, Hannah," her mother would shout.

"I won't," the child replied, the door popping behind her as she headed for her cedar tree.

Once inside, Hannah remembers the house as bigger somehow. Maybe the size of the old door her daddy brought home to close off the attic shrinks the other rooms. The sour smell of hay against the walls makes her sneeze. Other than the remembered size and the present owner making the place into a storage barn, not much has changed since the family moved away some thirty years earlier.

She glances back through the open door. Grief at the sight of what the tornado did to her knowing tree, the brutality of the storm lashing out against her cedar, hits her harder than having hay left in the house.

## Clifton Young's Door

With no neighbor for half a mile, the child Hannah plays alone or, when she could sneak one in, with a beagle pup from her daddy's dog pen outside her bedroom window.

"No dogs in this house," Maggie tells Hannah, edging the dog back out the door with her foot. "I won't live like white trash."

"We'll play in the attic. That's not really the house."

191

From one bedroom, an attic stairwell no more than a two-foot wide warped ladder, leads almost straight up.

"You stay out of there. You don't know what's up there. Fall down those stairs, you'll break your neck."

Nights in bed, Hannah listens to Maggie badger Carl. "I want a door," she says. "I build a fire all the heat goes up that stairwell hole. The stairs are so steep Hannah could get hurt. And me out here by myself."

"I'll take care of it," he promises. But he does not.

After a month, or maybe a year, it seems to Hannah, of listening to late night hounding, Carl nails a quilt over the door frame.

Maggie glares at the bright calico log cabin pattern attached to the wall with four-inch nails, her eyes flashing fire newly doused with kerosene. "It's one thing living in a house attached to a dog pen. It's another having a quilt for a door. You expect me to set food before your friends' wives and have them go home to talk about me having a ratty quilt for a door?"

Maggie has a look on her face that says she feels like Hannah does when she has long been unhappy about something she's done.

"It's a fine quilt. Made by my own mama. 'Sides, times, they're hard, Hon."

"Not so hard you can't find money for another hound." Maggie paces the pine plank floor.

"That's trading. No money passes hands."

"You're so good at trading, trade up a door. I won't have those women in here till I have a door over that hole. I never lived without a door in my life."

"You got a house with electricity. That's more'n most."

The next night Carl brings in the door. Taken from Clifton Young's corn crib, it is heavy and old, four hewn

192

planks. Splintery boards across the top and bottom hold it together.

Clifton Young helps haul it in and prop it against the stairwell door frame.

"Here's your door, Maggie," Carl huffs. He nods thanks to Clifton Young. "Cliff," he says, lowering his eyes. Clifton Young steps outside to smoke. Carl follows.

Hannah and Maggie look at the uneven weathered slabs. An angled hole marks where a hemp rope dropped at one time.

Hannah sees a touch of the empty look that appears in her mother's eyes whenever her daddy leaves with men for a hunt, but this time it is different in a way she doesn't recognize. Something deeper inside.

Angled on the wall, the door, too tall for the frame, rests against the ceiling and covers the attic opening, except for a shadowy space at the floor. From where Hannah stands, the gap looks like the dark under the lean-to back of the barn.

"Not even a house door," Maggie whispers to the floor.

Hannah is scared her mother might cry. She steps forward to take her thin hand.

Maggie turns away to face Carl as he comes back in.

"How'll you size it down?" Maggie looks eye to eye at Carl.

"I'll take care of it." He walks back out, slamming the screen behind him.

"It'll be okay, Mama." Hannah reaches again for her mother's hand.

With both hands against her side, Maggie stares at the screen door. To Hannah, she's reed-thin, too easily broken to handle big door problems.

193

"Look," Hannah points. "A playhouse." But Maggie has slipped her arms inside her apron bib and crossed them, leaving a hard fist showing on each side.

Turning in a swish, Maggie says, "Stay away," and stomps into the kitchen.

Now alone, the door hovers over Hannah like a screech owl, waiting for its prey to flinch.

That spring and summer Hannah watches Maggie watch the door. Her mother moves with a set mouth. Her breath comes out in grunts and her words in growls. When she mops, she sloshes soapy water against the walls. When she irons, she mashes the iron into the clothes. Whenever she walks through the room, she eyes the door, as if she expects it to step away from the frame and engulf the room.

From time to time, Maggie stops reading to Hannah and glowers at the door. "You stay away from there, you hear?"

Hannah blinks up at her mother, not knowing what to say or why her mother hates the door, for it has come to fascinate Hannah. Braced against the wall, it makes a perfect hidey-hole.

Mondays, while Maggie washes clothes on the back stoop, Hannah plays under the door. It becomes her own cave where she can be a bear or a fox or a panther and nobody knows. She has a dim room where her mother's voice never enters. There, she is braver than any bogeyman her mother has said hides in the attic since the coming of the door.

Hannah listens for Maggie to step up on the back porch after hanging clothes, and rather than risk a switching, she slips out of the darkness under the door. Maggie finds her in the middle of the room playing with her doll or under her cedar drawing lines in the dirt with a stick.

The stench of molding hay jars Hannah back to the here and now. She remembers she has her own child to see to. But instead of leaving, her old bedroom draws her to the right. She steps over loose hay and into the room that once butted against the dog pen, the room where she slept as a child.

Outside, Carl's beagles lived in a square, where a chicken wire fence and the jerry-rigged kitchen shaped the house into an ell. Out the back window, a field of beige broom sedge grows where the old barn had been. The tornado of '66 left little in the back but a gray corner post of the dog pen and rusted metal Ts holding Maggie's clothesline. The line, still intact, cuts a slack waver across the sky.

For a time, this room had been her parents' room. It was here the lace curtain first hung. Hannah marks where the bed stood, the wardrobe, her daddy's straight chair where he threw his plaid wool jacket winter nights. The chair where he could no longer leave his work boots and socks once Blackie came. Her parents slept here for a time, but Maggie couldn't stand the thumping against the wooden sleep boxes when dogs scratched themselves in the night.

"Do something with those hounds, Carl." Maggie talks lines across her forehead morning after morning.

"Now, Maggie, you know better. A dog's got to scratch. Just like a man's got man-things to do." Her daddy chuckles and pulls on his Lucky Strike.

"Stop that talking dirty." Maggie ducks her head. "I mean it." She looks up at Carl and steps away. "I've never lived with a passel of dogs outside my window. Back home, I was accustomed to nice things. Like lace and pretty hats. And soft nylons. Dogs drive me crazy. You've got to move that pen."

Hannah rotates a tawny braid around her finger, angling it out from her head.

"Don't pull your hair, Hannah," Maggie says, fingering her own. "It'll all fall out."

"They're staying right where they are, Hon. Kitchen knocks off the wind. Bedroom gives 'em shade. Hannah don't mind my dogs. Right, girl?" He draws her to him. "We'll move to the other room. Hannah'll sleep next to the pen."

Maggie takes down her lace curtain and hangs it in the adjoining room, the room that had been Hannah's. And Hannah moves in wall-to-wall with the hounds.

## A Dog in the House

After the attic and the boogolly, the beagles and their noise comfort Hannah. Having them outside her window, she knows a boogolly won't stand a chance against a good hunting hound. With the door to the front porch, one to her parents' bedroom, and a window to the west, she lies on her bed with her head against the one solid northern wall, propping herself on her pillow so she can watch the three entrances against the boogolly coming in. Nights, the eastern moon behind her cedar tree, she climbs out the window, selects a quiet puppy, lifts it by the nape of its neck, and brings it in.

Next morning, finding a dog asleep under the quilt, Maggie sends Hannah out back of the barn for a peach tree limb.

"Good nubs on peach," Maggie vows, "or whipping's not worth the effort."

Having a pup with her through the night means more to Hannah than a switching. When the limb starts its swishing zing, Hannah sends her own knowing self into the top of the big rusty cedar. There it waits on a branch till the lashing stops. Then it swirls down, filling itself as it drops with the tangy fir smell.

She's been deliberately disobedience. Her mother is going crazy. She has told Hannah so, and it's all Hannah's fault. That weight settles on Hannah with the heaviness of a folded woolen quilt mid-summer, yet lifts with the moist breath of a pup on her chest. Such suffering countered by relief makes for an uneasy calm.

Saturday nights, the men meet in a hunter's front yard with their dogs and their best liquor. Wives sometimes visit other wives, moving from house to house each week, while the men go to the woods.

Occasionally, a hunter shows up with a woman, but she knows to stay in whatever truck brought her as she'll be going into the woods herself.

Hannah has seen such a woman. She looked the same as the wives. Hannah had expected her to stand high in the air, taller than the men's trucks. She appeared to be no more than the shadow of a face inside a truck window. After Maggie continued to call her a painted woman, Hannah had hoped the woman would have graphic colorful designs across her face, exact details where she had managed with practice to color inside the lines.

Sunday mornings after, Maggie sends Hannah down the hill to draw well water. Hannah dips the tin bucket into the well pit and listens to her mother's voice slide down the incline. Even under the hill, she hears her mother carrying on against her daddy.

"I'll not have it, Carl. Some painted-up whore trying to act like a lady right in my own front yard. Just waiting for God knows what." Maggie stands in the middle of the room, her back to Hannah, who waits, bucket half-full in her hand, outside the screen.

"You can't say to a man what a man can and can't do." Carl rubs two fingers across his forehead. Rubbing his face makes talking to her mother easier, Hannah decides.

"This is your place. Tell him he can't bring her on your land."

"We're not so long in being here, Maggie." His voice sounds like the end of a long day at work. "Besides, you can't fault a man his choice in women."

"And liquor's another thing." She's walking back and forth across the room. "Clifton Young's no more than a flat-out drunk. He and that wife of his live off him running moonshine through these hills. I don't want him around Hannah."

"Then keep the girl in the house, damn it." Carl starts toward the kitchen.

"Come back here."

Hannah flies her own knowing self into her cedar. Now invisible, she takes a step back from the screen door.

Carl looks around at Hannah. Hannah tries to smile, but she's afraid her mouth goes up on the wrong side.

"Carl?" Maggie hangs back. "You never told me all this before I married you." Her voice cracks. "Weekend after weekend. It's always the same. You gone off on some hunt."

"I told you, once a dog man, always a dog man. If I recollect rightly, you said you'd have me." He turns back to Maggie, a grin much like Hannah's on his face.

"Being a dog man has to mean you're gone all the time? Me having to step over dog piles to get to my clothes line?" Maggie talks louder as Hannah's daddy speaks softer.

"Quieten down, Maggie. You're loud 'nough to frighten fox out their dens." Carl moves toward her into the floor ring of electric light from the bulb swaying on its plaited cord. "You're scaring the girl."

"Leave him alone, Mama." Hannah speaks through the screen.

Maggie faces Hannah with red in her eyes, "I sent you for water." Her voice cuts Hannah like a switch.

Maggie turns back to Carl, "Saying it and living it are two different things."

Carl edges out of the light and toward Maggie. "Aw, come on, Hon. Don't be mad. It's over and done. Saturday night's gone."

Maggie veers out of his way.

Hannah goes through the other porch door to her bedroom. Her dress is wet from the sloshing water, and she feels cold. Some Sundays Hannah doesn't bother to climb back up the hill till she hears her daddy's truck drive off.

## The Boogolly

Hannah sees the boogolly at week's beginning, a few months before she turns six. It's a hot Monday, a wash day.

While Maggie washes clothes out back, Hannah makes the cave under the door a playhouse for her doll. She whispers to the dolly and listens for a step on the porch. Heaviness on the board tells Hannah that Maggie has hung the last bed sheet. One footfall and Hannah pops out into the open.

Maggie walks in, her face red as cherries from facing summer heat and bending over iron wash pots of hot water. "It's miserable hot today. I'm going to the well and wash my hair," she says, her mouth crooked. "You stay put."

"Yes'm." Hannah winds the doll's handkerchief dress around her hand.

Maggie takes a jar of Pond's face cream and an Ivory soap bar, both the color of unleavened bread, off the dresser and leaves.

Hannah watches her go. When the top of her mother's head disappears under the hill, she picks up her book and reads the pictures to the doll. She finishes, puts down her doll, and wanders around the room, as if it's her first time there, running her fingers across slick white paint on the iron bedstead, down the wall, and over the dresser top. She lifts her mother's hairbrush, brushes the top of her head, smoothes back wild hairs that have escaped her two pigtails, and tightens cloth strips holding her braids. She rubs her palm across the lace pattern on her mother's curtain, then flattens in creases, so no one can tell she touched the fabric.

Behind her, the door to the attic waits, propped against the stairwell frame. Hannah creeps across the room. She bends a crooked half-moon at the waist and peeps out the front door. Her mother nowhere in sight, she tip-toes to the stairwell opening. At the foot of the stairs, she steals a look under Clifton Young's old door. A narrow shaft of pasty light slices into the far wall at the stairwell top.

Hannah lifts the quilt her mother has left hanging, crawls under and starts up the stairs. More ladder than stairs. She'd expected steps. Moving on hands and knees, she feels her way up. She'd expected more light. She had not thought of having to climb toward night in the middle of the day.

Inside, the stairwell smells like the underside of the house. Her footprints smear the dust, following her up the steps. On the top stair, Hannah stands up, and looks into the attic room's light to see if her daddy's yard dog might be here, his fur coated with his outdoorsy dirt smell.

No dog. Nothing moving.

200

Once she gets out of the stairwell and into the attic, it is easier to see wiggly shadows and stringy spider webs around the walls. A few cardboard boxes sit here and there around the walls. An old two-handled saw leans against a far wall. The ceiling slants on each side to leave room for the roof. Walls and ceiling are covered with slats, nailed so that cracks separate each from the other. Hannah finds herself standing halfway between the windows that open each end to the world outside. To her left through window dirt, she sees her own knowing cedar, quiet in the yard.

At the other end of the attic, light tries to come in the window, but a piece of old newspaper and more dirt shade the room. Little speckles of dust move in circles where stripes of light hit the sidewall.

Closed up oldness sneaks into her nose. She sneezes. And sneezes. And sneezes again. Hannah wipes the back of her hand across her nose, then onto her shorts. After a moment, she steps into the attic, as if entering an unexplored forest, one empty of cedars.

"Hannah."

Hannah whirls. Between her and the stairs stands a monster twice as high as Hannah is tall. Its face is floury white with black-circled eyes and mouth, its head covered with bubbles. Water drips down on its dress. It breathes hard.

"Boo," it says, quiet-like, and snorts, like it is drawing in air to pump itself up.

Hannah screams.

"Goll-ee," it whispers. "I knew I'd find you here."

Boogolly is all Hannah hears. She pushes past, going for the stairs.

"Wait." The boogolly sticks out a grabbing hand.

Hannah runs for the stair-ladder. She goes down face-forward, rather than climbing, skipping steps and

201

bumping her butt. At the bottom, she fights against the quilt. The sound of nails ripping through the quilt under the propped-up door is more powerful than the thud when she hits the floor. She doesn't stop until she throws herself against her cedar's trunk. Squeezing both arms around the tree, ignoring bark digging scratches into her skin, she flings her own knowing-self straight up to the safest top branch and leaves it there to forget what she has seen.

Somewhere in the distance, beyond the knowing tree, Hannah knows her mother is running, calling for her. She doesn't answer. Her mouth won't work.

Maggie finds Hannah sitting in dirt, plastered against the cedar.

"Hannah?"

Hannah looks past her mother, with her face slick and clean, her hair wet from its washing.

"Come inside, child."

"No," she mouths.

"Hannah? Look at me." Maggie lays her hand on Hannah's shoulder. "It's just me."

"No." She bends her body away from her mother, still grabbing the cedar with one hand, hugging the bark. "There's a boogolly in the attic," she says, her voice tiny, the tree holding her close.

"There's no such thing." Maggie loosens Hannah's hands from the trunk and lifts her up. The tree stays with her. Chips of brown bark poke from Hannah's fair arms.

"No. No." Hannah struggles against her mother. "I want my daddy." She sobs. Her nose runs.

"I told you not to be around that attic door." She puts Hannah back down. "Look at you. What a baby. You peed your pants. Get inside. I'll fix you."

"I want Daddy."

"Forget about this. You don't want your daddy to know what a whiner you are. 'Sides, your daddy's at work. He can't be here for you all the time."

Hannah waddles toward the house, her underpants heavy with caked dirt. Maggie follows, nudging her across the yard. Inside, Maggie picks bark out of Hannah's arms with a sewing needle and pours raw kerosene over the snags in Hannah's skin.

Hannah squeezes her eyes shut. She swallows the blood in her mouth from the bite that keeps her from screaming.

After the boogolly, Hannah doesn't sleep. She lies awake in her bed, wanting her daddy to grasp her in his arms and spin her round and round. But he sleeps in the room where the stairwell is—where her mother's lace curtain hangs—where sun patterns dance on the floor. She won't go in there in the dark.

At first, she cries out in the night.

"What's wrong with that girl?" her daddy asks.

"Just her imagination. She's scared of the attic. And a good thing, too."

"Linger a while with her. She's a baby yet," her daddy says. "Not even six."

Her mother lies with her nights until Hannah drifts off. One night Maggie comes in, and, instead of lying on the bed, she tucks the sheet tight around Hannah's neck and tells her, "I can't stay in here. I need to sleep in there. With your daddy. I won't be coming ever time you cry." She stands over Hannah like a dark door. "It's time you're a big girl." Maggie's wedding band clicks against the bed frame. She leaves Hannah alone.

Hannah lies awake, listening to a breeze in her cedar, long past the rising of the moon. The next night, as her daddy's beagles settle, Hannah climbs out the window and chooses a pup for sleeping.

## Blackie

Hannah turns six August 9, 1943. That afternoon, reading to her doll in the middle of the floor, she hears her daddy's heavy work boots step on the porch.

"Where's my birthday girl?" Coming into the room in a halo of cigarette smoke, Carl slams the front screen.

From the kitchen, Maggie snaps, "Carl. The screen door."

Hannah drops her doll and grabs him around his thighs. Carl holds his Sunday hat over her head, its felt bottom bulging with a load that puffs out its shape.

"What is it?" Hannah bounces, trying to touch the hat.

Maggie walks in from the kitchen, her arms chalky with flour. She crosses her arms and leans against the corner bedstead.

"You're ruining your good hat, Carl."

"It's Hannah's very own birthday present. Come outside and see for yourself." Her daddy's gray eyes shimmer like water off the roof when it breaks surface in the rain barrel at the corner of the house.

Hannah bounds to the front door and holds open the screen. Maggie marches out first, wiping her apron across her hands, then Carl, grinning and hiding the hat behind him. Hannah jumps off the porch and stands facing her mother and daddy, holding out both hands.

"Close your eyes," Carl says and places the hat in her hands.

Hannah opens her eyes and squeals. Red fur and two black eyes fill the hat. A fat chow chow puppy sticks out its black tongue and cleans its nose.

"Oh, Daddy. Oh, Daddy. My very own puppy." Hannah's eyes illuminate her face, and she laughs. "Come on." She tugs her daddy's hand. "Let's show him my tree. He needs to meet my tree." Hannah stumbles forward, her eyes fastened on the pup. "He has dark eyes like me. His name's 'Blackie'. Yes, it's Blackie. Hey, Blackie." She nuzzles her face into his fur.

"But he's red." Her father laughs out the words as the three move toward Hannah's cedar.

Maggie stays put on the porch.

The cedar's branches pull breezes out of the air, soften Hannah, her daddy, and Blackie in their twirling, and send them back down where the two sit together, shaded, the pup in Hannah's lap.

"His tongue, Daddy. See. It's black." The pup licks her hand to prove it is true. "And his eyes are black. Just like mine." Hannah giggles at the tongue's rough touch. "Look. He's kissing me. He loves me." It's then she grasps the significance of having her own pup in her own room. "He'll keep the boogolly away."

"Where'd you hear that, girl?" Her daddy frowns. "There's no such thing."

But her daddy hadn't been there.


"Not another dog," Maggie says from the porch, her hands on her hips.

"It's just a pup, Hon. It'll keep her out of your hair."

"She'll have it in the house."

"No, she won't. Will you, girl? I brought it a box crate for sleeping outside her door." He smiles. "Besides, he's one good dog. I know my dogs."

205

"Dogs in the front and dogs in the back. My God, Carl." Maggie walks in the house and slams the screen. From inside, she says, "The two of you are driving me crazy."

Hannah looks across to Carl. "Mama slammed the screen."

"We best not take him inside. Seems your mother don't approve."

Blackie scratches against the screen as soon as Hannah comes to bed. She cracks the door and lets him in, to sleep under her sheet.

The next morning Maggie switches Hannah's legs.

Blackie whimpers to come in the next night. Hannah lets him in.

The next morning Maggie switches Hannah's legs.

By the end of a week of switching, at supper Carl asks Maggie about the whelps on Hannah's body.

"She won't mind a word I say. Bringing that dog in every night. Switching does no good. I've never seen such a stubborn child." She glares across the table at Hannah.

"Why not let her be?"

"What? And let some dog live in my house?"

"Why not? The dog's clean enough. He stays right under her feet all day. Seems to reason he'd want to come in at night." Carl moves his chair closer to Maggie and lowers his voice. "If you let the dog come in with the girl, I'll see if I can't get Clifton to round you up some nice pairs of nylons."

The nylons will arrive after a month of hunts. Maggie will hang them, like two long worms, over the curtain rod, so she can see them move in the wind with her lace curtain. "But out that dog goes when company comes."

Before the next week is over, Blackie has taken the run of the house. He tries to pull Maggie's wash off the clothesline. She runs after him with the fly swatter she keeps ready for Hannah. Blackie outruns her.

Blackie bites into Carl's work socks. His puppy rumblings bring Hannah to the sock's rescue. Blackie worries the sock back and forth. Hannah catches the toe and pulls. Blackie's teeth cut a narrow gash from ankle to top before he turns loose. Blackie moves on to Carl's work boots. He gnaws the top into a fray. That night, Carl glues the leather back into place as best he can.

Hannah tries to keep him busy with a piece of rope. Tugging and tossing keep him happy a short time. Playing chase around Hannah's tree works for a while. He is his most gentle dashing about and sleeping with Hannah.

## The Wives

When nights turn cool, hunters draw long shadows across the ground as they squat around a short fire they've built in a tin foot tub. Somebody will have wrapped rags around the handle so he can lift the tub into a pickup bed and carry it into the woods. Guardians of the land, the men pride themselves in not firing fields or pines, in keeping safe rabbits and coons they send dogs in to tree.

Inside, wives circle a coal stove and mutter this and that while they do their stitching.

Early on, Maggie takes Hannah to the houses while she waits for Carl to run the dogs, but Hannah's restlessness bothers Mrs. Zula Harbison.

"Child's got ants in her britches. Can't you keep her still, girlie?" Mrs. Harbison speaks to Maggie.

"Carl says she's just feisty, Mrs. Harbison. That's all. Come over here, Hannah, and sit with Mama." She taps the edge of her chair. "Don't be running round like some wild animal."

Hannah sits on the floor next to her mother's feet. After a moment she tries to get up, but Maggie pulls her down by the dress tail and whispers in her ear.

"Sit still. Mrs. Harbison's got boogers tucked upstairs."

Hannah criss-crosses her legs and sits stone still. After a time, she draws finger figures of Blackie and her knowing tree on the linoleum floor.

Carl has told Maggie she needs to dig out a place for her and Hannah with the wives. She goes round and round with herself, talking aloud in front of Hannah, before she settles.

The next Saturday night, Maggie turns to the other wives waiting out the hunt. "I'd be pleased if you ladies'd come by our house." Maggie pauses. "Next week, maybe," she pauses again.

The others stop their work and look at her.

"We'll have coffee. And visit." She glances down to Hannah. "While Hannah sleeps."

Nobody answers.

Hannah thinks, if the women were her daddy's dogs, a fight might break out. The way they're sizing each other up. She moves in. "My mama's not really going crazy. It's just me." Hannah feels her mother's stare in the top of her head. "You can see my puppy. And my tree. And my mama's lace curtain."

Maggie kicks Hannah in the backside. "Shut up, child."

Going home, Maggie tells Carl about the invitation, leaving out what Hannah had said and her kick.

"After all you've bad-mouthed them women and their men and you're asking them to come to our house?"

"I'll make it sort of a party. Just Hannah and me, I get lonesome out here. Besides, if I'm stuck out here I might as well try to belong."

"Saying I shouldn't of married me a city girl?"

"Stop that." She runs her finger down Carl's arm and laughs. "The wives can sew. Mrs. Harbison said herself it's bound to be easier under the light bulb than her kerosene lamp. It'll keep Hannah out of trouble."

"Men gather where they gather." The truck hits a rut, shifting the dog box in the truck bed. "I don't have much say. I'll put it to them, but don't get your hopes up none."

Saturday, Maggie uses the last of her sugar stamps, and she and Hannah bake cookies for the wives. The men meet at the Harbison's place.

"Going to Harbison's?" Carl asks.

"No." Maggie's dogged stubbornness keeps her home with Hannah. "I've got my pride," she tells Carl.

"Don't take it personal, Hon. Give them time. Some folk don't take easy to newcomers."

After Carl leaves to meet the hunters, Hannah asks her mother if they can eat the cookies.

"I don't care what you do." Maggie goes into the kitchen.

Hannah and her handkerchief doll eat cookies on the bed, ever careful not to leave crumbs in case a mouse comes in the night. She takes three cookies out to Blackie. Before Hannah goes to sleep, she creeps into the next room. Maggie is still sitting at the kitchen table.

The next Saturday night, Carl leaves Hannah and Maggie at Mrs. Carter Young's. As the wives stitch in the parlor, Mrs. Carter Young crosses her legs. Hannah notices an inside fire blush her mother's face as she stares at Mrs. Young's lacy slip.

Maggie invites the wives again.

Friday, Maggie washes the damask tablecloth her mother gave her as a wedding present. She dips it in starch and hangs it on the clothesline by the dog pen, the sun drying it so stiff it can stand alone.

Hannah wants to lean it against the wall to see how straight it can be, but Maggie won't let her touch it.

"If Carter Young's wife can have fine lace on her petticoat, I can afford a stiff tablecloth," she tells Hannah.

Maggie sprinkles the cloth by hand, rolls it into a smooth ball, and puts it in the icebox. Saturday morning she heats the iron, folds the cloth in the center, and creases it in half. She turns it over, folding both edges to the centerline and irons in two more creases.

"I saw a tablecloth once in Richmond, all slick and ribbed like this," she says, slapping the iron down on the cloth with a plop. "In all the best restaurants, tablecloths are laundered, not washed, Hannah. Look close so you'll remember when you have wives over." Maggie pushes into the iron, the wooden board bending under pressure.

Hannah watches from a distance.

Maggie washes the lace curtain by hand and spreads it over the table to dry smooth. "All proper homes hang lace in their windows," she tells Hannah as she works.

They clean the three rooms. Hannah grinds coffee beans and spreads butter on loaf bread sandwiches. Maggie stirs the pound cake.

Early afternoon, Maggie hands Hannah an empty mason jar and sends her with a butcher knife to collect flowers off the side of the road. "We'll have flowers. None of the wives have had flowers." She calls out as Hannah leaves, "Stay on the road."

Down the road, Hannah, with Blackie trotting behind, finds a low area across the ditch. She jumps the ditch and gathers black-eyed susans and chicory. She loves chicory's clear blueness, though its leaves leave her hands stingy. Leaving Blackie on the road barking, she crosses into the bog, scaring a turtle who disappears from his sunning spot into the water. She walks a log into the mush, willing herself to move ever so lightly so the log won't roll. Steadying herself, she reaches up and cuts blossoms off sweet joe-pye weed. She puts the purple bloom to her nose and smells its vanilla scent, a smell comfortable as warm cake fresh out of the oven. Scooping up bog water, she sticks the weed blooms into her jar.

Back home, she finds the kitchen table in middle of the bedroom where the stair-ladder still hides behind the quilt. Maggie has the table centered under the light bulb and covered with the damask cloth. Shadows of swiggly black-green ivy show through the damask.

"I see the oil cloth coming through, Mama."

"It pads against the table crack. Don't say it and maybe they won't notice."

Maggie sets the jar of wild flowers in the middle of the table. She takes a scrap of flour sack she has dyed the color of sky and drapes it around the jar's mouth so the lid ripples don't show. Some blooms are beginning to wilt. Hannah tries without success to make them stand straight. The light, its bulb swaying, illuminates the tablecloth, with its woven roses, and floats them above the damask. Three parallel ridges run the length of the table and drop off the edge, setting up low, spiny hills like those back of the barn.

The piece of white lace Maggie's sister mailed in from Savannah hangs over the narrow-paned window beside the bed. Sunlight enlarges and copies its pattern over the floor like faded gray and cream carpet.

"It's beautiful, Mama." Hannah senses electrified air, generated by her mother's quiet excitement, rather than the clear bulb overhead.

"It'll have to do."

Hannah sits on the floor and traces the lace pattern on a piece of paper. She takes it into her bedroom and stands it in the window next to the dog pen. The paper bends and slides to the floor. She sneaks Blackie in. He attacks, growling puppy growls, and rips strips away the tracing paper.

When the women arrive, Maggie puts on a tight smile and boils a pot of coffee garnered from her coffee coupons. There will be a time without coffee, a time without tires and gasoline, a time when The War demands country over family. But that time comes as gradually as hunters leave Carl Stallworth's yard.

In the front yard, the ritual begins. Men park their trucks in a circle, alternating beds toward the road, so beagles in wire-faced boxes in the back wouldn't yap at each other. Voices hum, interrupted only by whittled cow horns yahooing the leaving signal to hunters across the hollow. When the echo stops, another horn answers. Some hunter loads the fire. Men crank their trucks and pull out.

Hannah watches from her bedroom door until, straining against rising night sounds, she can no longer hear dog boxes scrape against metal truck beds as tires bump down the riprap road.

Clifton Young's door falls on this Saturday night, the night the wives accept Maggie's invitation. Sitting round the kitchen table in the bedroom, the wives have commented on how ridges in the damask stand up on their own and how none have seen such lovely lace as that piece hanging on the window.

Taking it all in through the board crack in her door, Hannah almost speaks aloud. They hadn't see the floor design it'd made earlier.

They have eaten the butter sandwiches, and Maggie, her hair glistening clean under the light bulb, stands, holding the knife, ready for cutting pound cake.

"Be so thankful when we get juice out our way," Clifton Young's wife says. "Makes the day longer having more light. Gives a body more time to get her work done." She nods as if confirming her own truth.

"I hear tell the whole of east Tennessee has juice. Somebody named TVA strung it up," says Mrs. Zula Harbison, cocking her head. "You're the lucky one, girlie, young as you are, having electricity and all. It'll be 1950 or better, 'fore we get it out our way."

Old Mrs. Jessie says nothing, her gums working, waiting for her slice of cake.

"Yes, Carl and I are blessed," Maggie says. The butcher knife pings as it hit the plate under the cake. "Would you care for honey on your cake?"

With sundown upon them, with the hunters, their dogs, gone, Blackie whines and scratches his box. Hannah reaches through the door without making a sound, slips him out, and brings him inside. She sets him down on her bed and wraps one of her daddy's shirts around him, buttoning him up inside like a man and begins combing his feathery tail.

With the first tug, Blackie jerks away, wiggling his way out through the sleeve, and heads for the edge of the bed. Hannah caches his ear, pulling him back. Blackie yips, snaps at her hand, and darts for the next room, Hannah behind him.

Hearing noises, Maggie throws open the door and steps into the frame, blocking Hannah's chase. The little red chow dashes between Maggie's legs and under the table, bumping the leg and jiggling the weed blooms. A black-eyed susan drops onto the damask cloth.

"Hannah Stallworth, what will these ladies think? Having a dog in the house." She turns and smiles a straight-lipped smile at the wives watching her.

Hannah bobs left and right, around her mother's skirt, trying to spot Blackie. "But he's a good dog, Mama."

Mrs. Zula Harbison lifts her feet off the floor, her toes pointed toward the ceiling. Old Mrs. Jessie just chews.

Looking for a way out, the puppy runs to the front door, then the kitchen door, both closed. As Hannah edges past her mother, Maggie whispers into her ear, "Get that dog out of my house." Then aloud, "We'll see about this later, young lady."

The puppy darts behind the bed and comes out with Carl's dingy sock in its mouth. Clifton Young's wife giggles. Hannah dives for the puppy and misses.

"A lively pair you have here, dearie." Mrs. Zula Harbison clears her throat and lowers her feet.

"This is very unusual, Mrs. Harbison. We never have dogs in the house. Carl wouldn't stand for it, and I agree with him completely. But you know how children are." Maggie picks up a dishrag and lifts the coffee pot off the coal heater. "Can I pour you some more coffee?" Maggie stands over Mrs. Harbison. Clifton Young's wife has her hand over her mouth, but Hannah sees the snicker in her eyes.

"Hannah, don't chase that dog," her mother commands, as she fills Mrs. Zula Harbison's cup. "Stand still. Let him come to you. And put him out. Now!"

"It is a cute dog, I'd say. Haven't I seen dogs like that down in the colored quarters, Zula?" Clifton Young's wife speaks through her fingers.

"I wouldn't know, not being one to go there myself." Mrs. Harbison lifts her coffee cup. "Do you have milk, honey?"

"Seems like a good enough dog to me." Old enough to talk with her mouth full, Mrs. Jessie never quits chewing.

The puppy hurls himself through the only opening left in the room, the opening under the door leading to the attic. Hannah shoots in after him.

"Hannah Stallworth, come back here," Maggie yells.

Blackie's claws click against the wood as he lopes up the stairs.

"Blackie! No!" Hannah screams. "The boogolly!"

When he reaches the top, Blackie turns back and passes Hannah coming up. In the shadows, Hannah could barely see him, but she hears him panting from whatever he's seen at the head of the stairs. She chases him back down the stairwell. At the bottom of the stairs, he jumps the last two steps and bumps the corner of the door when he hits the floor, Hannah directly behind him.

Blackie yelps in pain when Maggie kicks him, bouncing him into the bottom of the door.

Hannah misses a step. Her feet fly out from under her. The door slides, bottom first into the room. Hannah falls forward, the door's top edge slicing across her mouth.

After her awakening, she raises herself up by her rear-end. Before her, a saucer-sized splat of blood puddles where she landed. Hannah squats on her knees, cotton panties stuck in the air, blood dripping from her lips. Three of her teeth lay on the floor, white dots in a growing red circle. They reflect light from the overhead bulb like the tiny pearls Carl will give her for her sixteenth birthday. Seeing her own blood, she cries out for her daddy.

Maggie yells for Carl. The wives pick up their sewing and scramble for the door like old hens trapped with a fox in the chicken pen. They flutter past Carl on his way in. Blackie dashes through the open screen, headed for the yard.

"Get that dog out of my house!" she spits at Carl as she stoops down by Hannah. "Oh my God. What have you done to this baby?"

Maggie glares up at Carl and snaps, "You and your blessed dogs."

Frightened by the despair in her mother's wail, Hannah clasps her hand over her mouth and cries as blood seeps through her fingers.

The door to the attic isn't here anymore. Her daddy took it away the night it fell. After the hunters and their wives pulled out of the yard, he loaded it himself. Put it in the back of the truck and didn't come back till late Sunday night.

Hannah now looks around the aged attic. Someone has torn cardboard off the far window, exposing jagged glass. Distorted by old glass and windowpane grime, Hannah looks at her reflection. Still, at forty-six she sees her scarred lip first, as if it's the only feature her face contains. She runs her finger over the indentation and wets her upper lip with her tongue. Once full, the lip now flattens out thin, with a hint of dip at the corners. Yes, she thinks, emptying herself of a sigh that sounds like a forced puff of air, things do tend toward change.

The fine line on her upper lip zigzags toward her nose. She sees it every time she fixes her face, even though a make-up specialist once assured her that foundation covers scars. People never mention it, but she sees their eyes bounce off it when they talk to her face to face. And she hears her mother say what she said every time she scrubbed Hannah's face or washed Hannah's hair, "I still can't believe your own daddy did this to you."

"He didn't mean to, Mama," Hannah would reply.

A few months and Blackie disappears. Hannah, sitting with her head laid against the door, listens to voices from the next room. Indistinct at first, the rage of her daddy strengthens against Maggie.

"That pup chewed up everything in the house. Your socks. Your shoes. Even my monthly rags. Whatever he could reach." It gets so quiet Hannah thinks her mother must have left the room.

"But the dog bounded up against the waving of my lace curtain. He yanked it down, bringing down the nylons you gave me. It shredded them. He worried my lace into worthless strips.

"I wouldn't hurt the dog. Not on purpose. I just picked up whatever was closest to swat the dog off my curtain. It wasn't until the pup yipped and fell that I realized I . . . "

"Had the stove poker." Carl finished for her.

Hannah heard her mother crying. She put her hand on the door to go in and soothe her, to tell her it was going to be all right. Carl's voice stopped her.

"I can see no reason for leaving the pup to suffer all day with a broken back, to suffer till I got home. You hit it once, you could hit it again."

Another long quiet time.

In a tiny voice, Hannah barely recognized as her daddy's, he said, "How can I tell Hannah I had to put the pup down?"

"But I had no idea the pup was still alive when I put him on the back stoop," Maggie argued. "'Sides you don't have to tell her."

"That pup was Hannah's treasure. You knew that," Carl countered. "The child has no one but you about all day. Next you'll have me saw down her damn cedar tree. Well, it won't be. It just won't be."

Hannah hears her daddy stomp out through the kitchen. She crawls to her bed and cries herself into exhaustion.

The next morning she avoids looking at her mother. Carl takes her to the stoop where Blackie lies as contented as if he's sleeping. Together, they dig the grave behind the barn. Maggie brings out curtain strips, folded small to fit around the pup, and tells Hannah she can wrap Blackie in the lace.

Hannah questions her mother with her eyes, but neither speaks. Maggie leaves them to the burial.

"Good dogs wait at the end of the rainbow when they die," Carl tells Hannah to stifle her crying. "They wait as long as they need to take their masters to the other side."

Hannah cannot lift her head.

"Blackie's there, Hannah, waiting for you." Her daddy rests his hand on her head. "He'd never let you down."

Carl leaves his daughter sitting by Blackie's grave. Hannah covers the mound with a tiny forest of cedar branches she sticks into the soft soil.

Looking past the window, toward where the old barn used to be, Hannah can't decide exactly where her daddy buried Blackie. None of the cedar sprouts took root. Not that she expected them to. Without something to give her reference, everything outside the house seems to run together.

The bog's still there. Beyond it and the next hill, the sun flings strips of rainbow-tinted ribbons across the sky, tying up the day so evening can settle in for the night. Behind her, the attic is vacant. Watching the sun resting on the lower ledge of the sky, Hannah remembers she has a stop yet to make before home.

From her place at the window, she looks one last time across the yard below. There, Hannah watches Maggie, a young wife again, step out of the house's shadow. A damp towel wrapped around her head, Maggie straightens the bow in the clothesline, moving the forked pole away from where it crimps the bed sheet. She tugs against the wet weight and a rising breeze, tilting her turban with the strain.

Blackie dashes from under the house, grabs a sheet corner, and swings himself forward. Maggie pulls him away. Carl appears around the corner, with Hannah, still six, holding his hand. They walk up behind Maggie. Carl drops Hannah's hand and slips his arm over Maggie's shoulder. Maggie lifts her face and kisses him on the mouth. The little girl standing on the other side puts her arm around her mother's waist, and Blackie sits at the child's feet. Breezes from her knowing tree toss sheets about like white flags. Their swaying teases Blackie into bounding upward trying to catch a corner. Hannah holds him back.

Their backs face Hannah, yet here in her attic, she knows each more intimately than she's ever known anyone before.


## The Aftermath

Through the broken window, a breeze lifts a salt and pepper spiral of hair from her forehead, bringing with it the combined smells of old cedar and the vanilla of warm sugar cookies. With the scents, the boogolly, a towel draped shawl-like over its shoulders, emerges from attic shadows with the grace of a swaying tree branch and washes over Hannah's own knowing self. It appears close, close enough for Hannah to touch. It whispers, "Here I am."

Hannah lifts the corner of the towel and wipes cold cream from its face. She examines the boogolly closely. "So. It's just you." She breathes easy. Hannah takes its face in her hands and speaks in a goodnight voice, "Don't worry, Mama. It'll be all right." In the distance, a beagle bays. "It'll be all right," she says.

Outside, Hannah drops into dirt at the base of her knowing tree's trunk. She presses her face into aged bark and flinches at the stench of cow manure. Within her, the cycle of what was, what is, and what might become draws tighter. When she slipped on the attic stair-ladder, she began a spiral down a cardboard-brown chute leading her to this point. She never sat comfortably at her mother's table, for not the door, not her daddy, had gashed her lip. But the boogolly. Leaving her mouth swollen speechless while her mother stood over the bed those recovering days and raged at Hannah for her numerous discretions.

Hannah understands why today she, in traveling to see her mother, circled back to the old Stallworth place. She turns toward the now colored on-coming dusk, eases herself through barbed wire, and heads toward Crossing's Convalescence Home to sit on the floor.

There at the wheel of her mother's chair, Hannah will linger, willing her mother to speak. Maggie haunted by a look of long regret will stare through yellowed lace curtains into the adjoining pines. Hannah will hug the chair's metal wheel, while she and her mother gaze beyond a sky tinged pink by some far-away island's volcanic eruption, watching, as if waiting for Carl's beagles to trot out, Carl following close behind.

## SHORT STORIES PUBLISHED AND PUBLISHERS:

"The Prodigal"—*Carve Magazine* (online)
"Hard as a Rock"—*Pithead Chapel* (online)
"Fishtales Told to a Crow Mid-Spring"—*Belles' Letters*; Livingston Press
"Moon Shadows Dancing"—*Marrs Field Journal*; University of Alabama, Tuscaloosa Campus
"A Widow's Mite"—Chattanooga Writers Guild
"Carter's Woman"—*Seven Hills Magazine*
"A Child Handed Down"—*Explorations Magazine*; University of Alaska
"Martha Louise's Story"—*Longleaf Style Magazine*
"Chicken Bone"—*Change Seven Magazine*
"That Which Passes"—*Belles' Letters 2*; Livingston Press
"Waiting for the Pink"—*Climbing Mt. Cheaha*; Livingston Press
"Boogollies, Lace Curtains and a Dog in the House" (Excerpt)—*Birmingham Arts Journal*
"Letter from Vicksburg"—*Longleaf Style Magazine*
"The Uncertainty of Light"—*Birmingham Arts Journal*

## SHORT STORY AWARDS

"Moon Shadows Dancing"—Scott and Zelda Fitzgerald Award
"A Widow's Mite"—Patricia Boatner Award; Tennessee Mountain Writers
"She" ("Carter's Woman")—H. E. Francis Award; University of Alabama, Huntsville Campus
"She" ("Carter's Woman")—Harriet Arnow Award for Short Stories – Appalachian Writers Association
"Waiting for the Pink"—Hackney Award; Birmingham Southern College

## About the Author

Laura Hunter is a retired educator and an insatiable reader. She has always wanted to write stories and began doing so before entering the first grade. Since 1994, she has published sixteen award-winning fiction pieces and nine poems in addition to numerous articles published through several different media outlets. Her debut novel *Beloved Mother* has won numerous awards that are noted on the next page. In her spare time, Hunter reads, gardens, and works with a small writing group in Tuscaloosa, Alabama. Her writings reflect the perseverance of the downtrodden; those who refuse to give up, even against extreme odds.

Laura would greatly appreciate feedback for her work to be left on Amazon, Goodreads, or any other of your favorite review platforms.

*Beloved Mother* is a braided narrative of three women striving for meaning in their lives amidst turmoil in their relationships and living conditions. Laura Hunter explores what happens when motherhood is not idyllic, but painful and full of regret.

**Awards won in 2019 by Beloved Mother**
Next Generation INDIE Book Award
Fiction Grand Prize
First Place Winner
First Novel (over 90,000 words)
Grand Prize Winner

American Fiction Awards
Best New Fiction
Finalist – Best Cover Design

Literary Titan Book Award
Literary Titan Silver Book Award

Foreword Reviews Award
General Adult Fiction (Finalist)
General Historical Fiction (Finalist)
(Final awards to be announced June 17)

**Praise for Beloved Mother**
Laura Hunter has created a world in which the land matters.
Set in Appalachia, her novel crosses regional boundaries that
include Native American traditions and industrial progress,
while exploring the timeless themes of greed, exploitation,
kinship, and family . . . Here, Hunter's love of story shows.
—Wendy Reed, author of *An Accidental Memoir*

*Beloved Mother* is an adventure story about three generations
of daring women. Hunter tells us that "women have within
them so much love and so much hate they sometime confuse
the two," one of the many mysteries about this fast-paced
novel that will keep you wondering.
— Denton Loving, author of *Crimes Against Birds*

www.ingramcontent.com/pod-product-compliance
Lightning Source LLC
Chambersburg PA
CBHW031947010726
47493CB00007B/2109